Lights . . . camera . . . cut?

"So how was Rita, Nancy?" Tripp asked as he pulled some dresses off the rack. "Totally hyper, I bet. She acts like the only reason the computers went down was to inconvenience her."

"If you ask me, it's kind of a blessing," Julie said, pinning up my hem.

"Blessing?" I repeated. "How do you mean?"

"This whole production was a mess long before this morning," she answered. "It's probably a good idea for everyone to stop and take a breath."

"But why?" I asked. "Aren't you just getting started? How could it be a mess already?"

NANCY DREW
girl detective™

Available from Aladdin Paperbacks

NANCY
DREW
girl detective ™

#5

Lights, Camera . . .

CAROLYN KEENE

Aladdin Paperbacks
New York   London   Toronto   Sydney

First Aladdin Paperbacks edition May 2004

Copyright © 2004 by Simon & Schuster, Inc.

ALADDIN PAPERBACKS
An imprint of Simon & Schuster Children's Publishing Division
1230 Avenue of the Americas, New York, NY 10020

Manufactured in the United States of America
20   19   18   17   16   15   14   13

NANCY DREW and colophon are registered trademarks of
Simon & Schuster, Inc.

NANCY DREW: GIRL DETECTIVE is a trademark of
Simon & Schuster, Inc.

Library of Congress Control Number 2003115226

ISBN-13: 978-0-689-86570-1 (Aladdin pbk.)
ISBN-10: 0-689-86570-8 (Aladdin pbk.)

Contents

There's Something in the Air

S hopping for clothes would never be my first choice of things to do on a perfectly beautiful Saturday afternoon. My name is Nancy Drew, and although my friend Bess Marvin might disagree, I'm not completely hopeless when it comes to fashion. But I'm not interested in wasting a lot of time on it either. Not when there are so many more exciting things to do.

Last Saturday was a perfect example. Bess and her cousin George Fayne—my best friends—and I had planned something for that day, although I honestly don't remember what it was now. But I know George needed new running shoes and insisted we shop for those first. So we headed to Step Up, the best sports shoe store in River Heights.

My presence was especially important because George was a little short of money, and I said I'd float her a loan. After all, what are best friends for?

George is a real athlete, so these shoes were important. I understood that, because I run too. But she and Bess found about a zillion ways to debate . . . well, argue . . . about the merits of one shoe over another! I drifted away from my friends and stood by the front window, looking out on downtown River Heights. Because the weather was so great, there were a lot of people strolling through the streets, skateboarding, and shopping.

". . . Don't you think, Nancy?" Bess asked from the other side of the store.

"She's not listening," George said before I could answer. "She's off in her own world."

Frankly I was beginning to feel a little caged in, and was wondering whether we'd *ever* get out of there. I felt rescued when I saw Luther Eldridge scurrying across the street. He's an expert in the history of River Heights and always has interesting stories to share. And he's also a good friend—so he can be counted on to jolt me out of a major boredom attack.

"Luther!" I called, stepping outside the store. He didn't seem to hear me, so I called to him again. This time he stopped abruptly and waved.

"Nancy, I'm glad to see you," he answered as he

hurried over to my side of the street. The bright sun highlighted the worried expression on his face.

"Have you heard about the movie?" he asked. "They're filming a movie here."

"Yes, isn't that great?" I answered. "Dad and I were talking about it last night. It's going to be a TV movie. Dad's doing some of the legal work for the location shots around the area. He couldn't tell me what the film's about, though. I guess it's confidential until the official announcement."

Luther looked around and then leaned in a little closer. "I know what it's about, Nancy," he said. "I just found out a little while ago. Sam Sherman's place down by the river is going to be one of the shooting locations, and he told me. It's about us!"

"Us? What do you mean?"

"It's going to be a reenactment of the Rackham Gang heist."

"Wow. I know that was a pretty famous crime around this area," I told him, "but I'm surprised that major movie producers know about it."

"Well, Morris Dunnowitz apparently does. He's a big Hollywood producer and director, and he heard the story somewhere."

"Cool. Luther, this is going to be really fun! When do they start shooting?"

"I don't know, but they're already starting to set up

camp. No matter when they start, it'll be *too* soon as far as I'm concerned. I don't think it's going to be fun at all. I think it'll be a disaster!"

"Why? It's an exciting story. I think it'll make a great movie."

"Yes, but sometimes moviemakers change the facts or add things," Luther pointed out. "They completely change history."

"I know," I agreed. "But maybe that won't happen this time."

"Well, I just don't see how an outsider like this Morris Dunnowitz—and whoever he's got writing the screenplay—could possibly know everything about that robbery. And that means the film won't be the true story."

"I know one way we can make sure the moviemakers get it right, Luther. They can hire you as a consultant. You've spent a lot of time uncovering all the facts about that case. Who better to make sure they have their facts straight? Where are they setting up camp?"

"About four miles out of town, on the bluff above Rocky Edge."

"So why don't you just go out there and offer your services? They might jump at the chance to have a local expert filling in some of the details."

"Yeah, or they might kick me out the door!"

I could tell Luther needed some support. "I'll go

with you," I offered. "Come on. It's worth a try."

A small smile creased Luther's face. I was really fired up, because hanging out on a movie set was a far better escape from shoe shopping than I could have thought up. "I'll be back in a minute," I told him.

I told Bess and George where I was going, handed George a wad of money, and told them that I'd be back in touch later. Then I rejoined Luther and we walked to his car. He drove out of town along River Road until we reached Rocky Edge, where the deep Muskoka River curves to the south.

"That's got to be it," I told Luther. I pointed to a group of trailers clustered on the bluff. A couple of unmarked moving vans were parked nearby, and a few people were strolling around from trailer to trailer. Luther pulled the car into a spot under a huge old sycamore. I was surprised to see there was no fence around the area, and no guards watching for trespassers.

"Okay," I said. "Let's go get you on the payroll."

A large metal building anchored the nearest end of the compound of trailers. The building's door was open, and it rocked a little on its hinges as the wind came up the side of the bluff from the river fifty yards below. A sign above the door announced OFFICE in red paint. I led Luther to the open door and peered inside the building.

The front room looked like a small office—a very

busy office. Three women and a man were working at separate desks. Fingers flew over computer keyboards, and voices babbled into headsets.

I gave Luther a gentle prod, and he stepped up to the first desk.

"I'm . . . I'm here to see Mr. Dunnowitz," he said in a soft voice. "Where might I find him?"

The girl at the desk never looked away from her computer screen or disconnected from her phone, but she managed to answer Luther. "Do you have an appointment?" she asked. "May I have your name?"

"No, I don't have an appointment," Luther said, his voice stronger and more forceful. "But it is imperative that I speak with him. If he can't see me now, could we just set a time when I can come back?"

The girl finally stopped typing and looked at Luther, then at me, then back at Luther. "Actually, he's out on the grounds somewhere. Just ask anyone where he is. Try the lighting trailer first. He's in a pretty good mood today. If you can find him, you can probably talk to him now." She turned back to her work.

Luther and I left the building and started toward the trailers. Small metal signs next to each door identified the activity inside: WARDROBE, MAKEUP, FIRST AID, COACHING.

At the far end of the compound stood two large temporary buildings. The doors of one were open, revealing a lot of activity inside. It was outfitted with metal and carpentry shops, and a half dozen trades-men were hard at work.

"There's the lighting trailer," I said. "Let's check it out."

Luther went to knock on the trailer door, but there was no response. I climbed up the three steps and pulled the door open.

"Hello," I said. "We're looking for Mr. Dunnowitz. We were told he might be here."

"He just left," someone called from the back room. "Try the sound studio."

A huge building had been constructed where all the movie's interior sets were being built. Luther knocked on the door, and this time someone an-swered with a friendly "come in."

The first room was filled with computers and electronic video machines and playbacks. Two men were huddled over a notebook full of handwritten pages dotted with simple drawings. They both looked startled to see us.

"You're not who we expected at all," said one man with a slight smile. "You must be new. When did you join the team?"

"That's what we're here to discuss," Luther said. "Is either of you Morris Dunnowitz?"

"I am," the other man said, walking toward us.

"This is my cinematographer, Lee Chang."

"I'm Luther Eldridge, and this is—"

"No!" Mr. Dunnowitz said, extending his hand for a shake. "That's uncanny. I've been trying to call you all afternoon! You've heard about our film, I'm sure. I'm the director, and I'm also producing it. Probably a dumb idea to do both, but I want to make sure it's done right. I love this story, and I want everyone to love it the way I do. Nothing like century-old crimes to grab an audience's attention. But you know that, don't you? I understand that you're sort of the resident historian for this splendid town. So are you ready to go to work for us? We really need you! In fact, I won't take no for an answer."

Mr. Dunnowitz finally stopped talking, and Luther seemed sort of dumbstruck. So I stepped in.

"That is *exactly* why we're here, Mr. Dunnowitz," I began. "Luther—"

"It's Morris," the director said, turning to smile warmly at me. "Please call me Morris."

"Morris," Luther said. "I came to talk to you about being hired on as a consultant. I really know the history behind—"

"Exactly," Morris said, interrupting the conversation again. "I've researched this town—every nook and cranny, every business and government office, every citizen. I know all about you, and would love

to have you on board—and we're prepared to make it worth your while." He named a figure that made Luther's eyes pop out a little in shock. It wasn't a really huge sum—but it was pretty huge for Luther. "Of course, if there are schedule extensions, you'll be paid more accordingly."

Luther and Morris shook hands again, this time to seal the deal.

"And you, young lady." Morris turned to me. "What's your story?" he asked. "Who are you?"

"This is Nancy Drew," Luther said. "She's—"

"The famous detective," Morris said. "Of course."

"You know who I am?" I asked.

"Of course," he explained. "Anyone who's studied River Heights is going to know about Nancy Drew. I hoped I'd meet you. Maybe we can find some time to talk while I'm here. You might have some other cases that we could turn into movies."

I was really surprised that he'd heard of me. In fact, it made me feel really good. But the best part was seeing Luther's beaming smile. I could tell he felt a lot better about the way the movie was going to be made.

"Let's get you a script, Luther," Morris said, striding to the door. "The screenplay was written by Althea Waters, and she's here on the set. I think you'll like each other. You'd better," he added, with a broad grin. "You'll be working pretty closely together for a while!"

Morris led Luther and me out of the building and across the compound.

"Speaking of working on the production," Morris said, "we plan to use some of the local residents as extras and even for some smaller roles. We're on a fairly tight budget, so the pay won't be outstanding, but it will be pretty good."

"What are you getting at?" Luther asked.

"Nancy, I think you'd be perfect in the role of Esther Rackham," Morris said.

"Yes!" Luther exclaimed. "Of course. The sister of the thieving Rackham boys. You know, Nancy—she's the one who tried to keep them from stealing the money. He's right—you'd be perfect."

"And she died without revealing anything she might have known about the fate of her brothers," Morris added. "It's a small role, but a juicy one, Nancy. Have you had any acting experience?"

"Not professionally," I told him. "I've done some local productions—in high school and in a community theater. I don't know . . ."

My heart was pounding. Actually the idea was really exciting. Me—in a real *movie*. But I wanted to think about it.

"Think about it," Morris said, as if he was reading my thoughts. "But I'd love to have you on board. After all, the movie's about the original mystery in

River Heights, and you're the town's most original detective. Here we are—the supply trailer."

He tried the door, but it wouldn't budge. Then he checked his watch.

"My supply chief must be on break," he told us. "We always keep this trailer locked if there's no one on duty inside. Fortunately, I have my own key."

We went inside, and Morris headed straight for a double-door closet at the front of the trailer. He opened the door. "Hmmm . . . the light's not working," he muttered. "It's supposed to go on when the door opens. Let me see. I think the scripts are stacked up here."

My eyes followed his arm as it reached up toward a deep shelf piled high with papers. Something flashed from the back of the shelf behind his hand. At first I thought it might be the automatic closet light, sputtering on after all. But then I saw the flashes again. Two of them, glinting yellow as they reflected the light from the room's fluorescent ceiling bulb.

My stomach turned over as my eyes got used to the dark at the back of the closet. A huge cat—or something—was lurking in the corner of the shelf.

"Morris!" I yelled. "Get back!"

With a flash of yellow eyes and sharp teeth, a large blob covered in long black hair lunged from the back of the shelf.

11

2

Bugged!

It wasn't a cat—it didn't take more than a second to find that out. When the hairy blob flew off the shelf toward Morris, the acrid stink of skunk spray filled the room.

A flurry of paper drifted from the shelf as the skunk skidded into the air. Morris ducked slightly, and his back became a landing pad on the skunk's path to escape. Morris reached around, waving his arms to bat off the intruder, but the skunk sank its incisors into Morris's hand.

While Luther ran over to help Morris, I reached back to open the trailer door. The sudden rush of fresh air lasted only a few seconds before it was completely obliterated by the pungent stench.

The skunk looked outside. Then, using its long

curved toenails for a painful push off, it leaped to the floor and scurried out the door.

Morris and Luther followed quickly. My eyes were burning from the putrid air, and I could hardly breathe, but something caught my eye as I turned to leave. Most of the papers that had shot from the shelf with the skunk looked the same, but one was very different. I reached down and grabbed it; then I hurried outside.

I knew from past experience that skunk spray can travel an amazing distance. Still, I was surprised at how far from the trailer we had to go before we got a slight whiff of clean air.

"Yeow!" Morris yelled, shaking his hand. "That hurts!" he added, flexing his fingers. Those nasty skunk teeth had left a row of puncture marks on the back of his hand, and it was already swelling and purplish red.

"Let's get over to the medical trailer right away," I urged him. "You need to get that cleaned up, and you'll probably need a rabies shot."

"I'm feeling kind of dizzy," Morris said, cradling his bleeding hand. He went back to lock the trailer. When he rejoined us, he was sweating and started to tremble as if he was chilled. "It hurts a lot."

"Let's go," I said. "I think you're starting to go into shock."

Luther and I propped Morris up and walked him to the first-aid trailer. The doctor and nurse were shocked when we told them what happened. They immediately went to work on their boss.

We started toward the door, but Morris called us back and asked us to stay. He was lying on a cot in the back room while the nurse took his vital signs.

Luther and I decided to stay for a little while. We sat on the banquette in the front room. While we waited, I checked in with Bess and George on my cell phone. I didn't go into any detail, but made plans to meet them later at Sylvio's for pizza.

"I saw you pick something up just before you ran out of the trailer," Luther told me. "What was it?"

"I'm not sure," I said. "I haven't looked at it myself." I reached into my pocket where I'd stuffed the piece of paper. "All the pages that fell off the shelf were typewritten except this one."

"Scripts," Morris mumbled from the back room. "I can hear you, but talk louder? Those were scripts that the skunk pulled down with him."

"Well, this page stood out because it *wasn't* typed," I said, raising my voice a little. I unfolded the page and smoothed it out.

Luther stole a quick glance. "It's handwritten," he observed.

"Exactly," I said, quickly scanning the page. "I'll read it to you. Morris, listen to this—the first and last lines are in capital letters:

THIS MOVIE STINKS!
Your camp,
with its noise,
surface damage, and waste,
endangers innocent creatures
like this one,
destroys the natural beauty,
and disrupts the ecology
of this river and its banks.
GET OUT!

"*Innocent* creature?" Morris said. "Take a look at this hand. Innocent creature, ha!"

Luther and I went into the back room. The nurse was finished. "Well, now, in all fairness," Luther said, "that skunk was just trying to defend itself."

"You're right, you're right," Morris said. "The real culprits are the ones who trapped the skunk and closed it up in the closet. *They're* the ones who were endangering a wild animal."

"Is the note signed?" Luther asked.

"It is," I answered. "Want to guess by whom?"

"Sure," Luther said. "The Muskoka Musketeers."

"The what?" Morris asked, sitting up. "The Muskoka what?"

"Musketeers," I answered.

"I know what the Muskoka is," Morris said, gesturing toward the window.

"Please lie still, Morris," the doctor said.

"And I know what a musketeer is," Morris said, ignoring the physician's order and swooping an imaginary sword through the air. "But what does a musketeer have to do with the river? Muskoka Musketeers sounds like a rock band but I'm betting from that note it's a group of environmentalists. Am I right?"

"You are," Luther said. "And I'm betting this won't be the last you'll hear from them."

"Morris, I want you to stay here for a half hour at least," the doctor said. "And I want you to lie quietly—no distractions," he added, looking over at Luther and me.

I could take the hint. "Come on," I said. "Let's get back to town and let him rest."

"Luther, on your way out, stop by the office and pick up your employment papers and ID," Morris said. "I'll let you know about when to report here. Your first assignment will be meeting our screenwriter, Althea. Oh, and please have Rita send one of

16

our security people over here. I want to find out how a Musketeer brandishing a skunk managed to get into a locked trailer."

"Morris—," the doctor began.

"I'd be glad to talk to the security officer for you while you rest, Morris," I broke in. "I can get some preliminary information at least, and I can alert the security staff that there's been a breach."

"Excellent idea, Nancy," he said, lying back on the cot. "Having the famous Nancy Drew as part of my security team . . . great idea . . . I need to keep you out here, anyway, so I can bug you to play Esther . . . perfect." Still mumbling, he drifted off to sleep. They must have given him a sedative.

Luther went to the office building to check in, and I strolled around the compound. I finally found a large trailer labeled SECURITY.

I knocked, and the door opened immediately. A young woman peeked out. Her nametag identified her as Jane Brandon. "Whoa, you must have been the girl who was with Morris when the skunk bit him," she said, resting her finger under her nose.

"You guessed it," I said, "although I'm sure my 'perfume' gave me away. Sorry about that. We can talk out here if you like, so I won't drag these fumes into the trailer."

"Good idea," she said, stepping outside. She closed

and locked the door, and walked down the steps to where I stood. "Don't be too self-conscious about the smell," she said. "I'm a farm girl—I've been around more than my share of skunks."

We walked along the bluff above the river. I told her that Morris had asked me to talk with her, and she seemed happy to hear that. "One of the first things that struck me when Luther and I arrived earlier was that you guys aren't fenced in at all," I said, "and no one is posted to keep out visitors. Morris seemed to be shocked that someone could just walk in with a skunk, but it didn't surprise me at all."

"There are only two of us in security so far," she explained. "Dave Linn and me. He's over at the supply trailer. This is a really low-budget operation. Morris has promised that when we actually begin shooting and the excitement really starts, we'll have more security people. But right now . . . he seems to think we don't need any more."

I told her about my background as a detective, and she seemed genuinely impressed and relieved.

"Frankly, we can use all the help we can get," she said. "This production has had a lot of trouble from the get-go, and I wouldn't be surprised if that animal didn't just crawl in there on his own."

"You're right." I showed her the note from the Muskoka Musketeers and told her what I knew about them. "Have you seen any reporters around? The Musketeers love publicity, so they might have alerted the press about what they had planned, so they could make the TV news tomorrow."

"No. No one from town seems to have gotten wind of it," she answered. We looked at each other and, smelling the pungent odor, broke into laughter at her unintentional joke. I had a good feeling about working with her. Sometimes professional security people don't like an outsider working on their cases. But Jane seemed to be really open to the idea.

"I'll be glad to talk to the Musketeers, if you like," I volunteered. "It's a local group. Chances are I know some of the members, and they might be more open to talking with me. I could set up a meeting between them and you and Morris. Maybe have Luther Eldridge sit in too. He's very well known around here as someone who's interested in protecting the history of River Heights. And Morris has just hired him as a script consultant—the Musketeers should like that."

"That sounds great," Jane said. "Try to get something going for tomorrow, will you? That will give Morris a chance to rest a little, and also give us time to jump into our investigation. Then we'll be primed for the meeting."

I agreed to her suggestion and started back to the office to track down Luther. He was there waiting for me, and he couldn't stop talking as we walked to his car. This was rare for him. I had met Luther through his daughter, who had been a friend of mine. She and the rest of his family were all killed in a car accident a few years ago. He's been almost a hermit ever since—so it was great to see him excited again.

Luther pulled his car out of the compound and we started back along the Muskoka toward River Heights. Even though it had been over an hour since the spraying, we both still stunk from the skunk.

"My car will never be the same," Luther said with a sigh. "Oh well, maybe it's time to trade it in anyway. Although I don't know anyone offhand who'd take it at this point."

"It'll air out eventually," I said, "in maybe ten years or so!"

We hadn't gone more than a couple of miles when I noticed a few small tents in a clearing ahead. "There they are," I pointed out. The Muskoka Musketeers had set up a small protest site on the riverbank. A half dozen people waved and held up signs as we zipped by.

"Do you want to stop?" Luther suggested. "We could walk all through the camp and stink up the place."

"Not now," I said, smirking. I told him about my conversation with Jane Brandon, and about setting up a meeting for the next day. "Besides, I don't want to give them the satisfaction of knowing their skunk ambush worked so well."

"Good idea," Luther said as he pulled into town. "Thank goodness they tend to be a pretty peaceful bunch. We should be able to work something out with them."

Before long we were turning onto Park Street. "I assume you want to go home," Luther said.

"Absolutely," I answered. "I'm supposed to meet Bess and George at Sylvio's, and there's no way I can go smelling like this."

After a few more minutes, Luther stopped his car in my driveway. "Well, thanks for another adventurous afternoon with Nancy Drew," he said. His grin crinkled his face into a dozen wrinkles. "So . . . I'll be seeing you on the set, right, Esther?"

"I said I'd think about it," I told him. "And I will." That was the truth. I really hadn't made up my mind yet.

I waved good-bye, then went inside to clean up. Well, at least I tried to. I was kind of glad no one was home to greet me. I live with my dad and our housekeeper, Hannah—my mom died when I was three. If Hannah had been home when I came in smelling like a skunk, I'd be cleaning up for weeks.

The thing about really bad smells is that they go

through your nose and up into your sinuses. Or maybe it's just such a shock to your senses, that it stays in your memory. All I know is I scrubbed for half an hour, and I couldn't tell whether it did any good or not. My head was still full of skunk stink.

I finally gave up and drove to Sylvio's. No one seemed to notice when I walked in. I figured that was a good sign. The waitress I walked by didn't hold her nose, and people didn't jump up and run out like they do in cartoons when a skunk walks in. I sat down with Bess and George at a table by the window.

"We didn't think you'd ever get here," Bess said. "Tell us everything—and don't leave anything out." She leaned in to hear my report. Bess is really pretty—blond, with perfect features. And right then, her perfect little nose began to twitch. She's also kind, and doesn't like to hurt people's feelings, so she didn't say anything. She just leaned back in her chair and casually rested her hand in front of her nose.

George, on the other hand, is very direct. "Where have you been?" she exclaimed. "Or should I ask, what have you been rolling in?"

I told my friends about my afternoon with Luther and Morris Dunnowitz.

"You're going to be *in* the movie?" Bess said, ignoring the part about the skunk. I knew she'd think working on the film was a great idea. And to be honest, just hearing the enthusiasm in her voice got me excited about it.

"Do you think you can do it?" George asked. "I've heard film acting can be pretty boring. A lot of waiting around, endless retakes. Besides, you haven't had any experience in something like that. Are you good enough to be in a real movie?"

"Of *course* she is," Bess pointed out. "She was Buttercup in *Pinafore,* and she was wonderful!"

"That was in the seventh grade," George reminded her cousin. "And she was all right—until she ran off the stage in the middle of Act Two, sick. Remember? I'm not sure that really counts."

"Who else is in it?" Bess asked, leaning across the table. "Who are the stars?"

"I have no idea," I said, "I don't really know anything about it except the story. Wouldn't Ned be great as one of the Rackham brothers? The camera would love his dimples. Too bad he left for that book fair in Chicago."

"But the part of Esther is small, right?" Bess asked. "Esther Rackham was the sister of the bad guys, wasn't she?"

"Yes," I answered. "If I remember the legend correctly, it should only be a couple of scenes."

"It's perfect," Bess declared. "The movie's about the most famous River Heights mystery, and it will star the most famous River Heights detective! You *have* to do it."

"That's just what the director said," I told her. "Except the word *star* is a little extreme. But it does seem to be a natural fit, personality-wise, doesn't it? Besides, this production is going to be really important to Luther. Playing this part will sort of be a way to support him." I paused, thinking about some of the other bit parts I had played in grade-school plays. I had been nervous every time—but I was older now. I would be able to handle it, right? "I guess I'll do it," I finally muttered.

While Bess and George dove into the pizza, I called Morris and told him my decision. Hesitant as I was, I was really happy to hear that he was feeling better, and that the accident with the skunk wasn't going to slow him or the filming down.

Bess, George, and I spent the rest of the evening talking about our favorite films and movie stars. When I told them that Morris was looking for extras and bit players, their eyes lit up at the prospect of seeing their own names in the credits.

Sunday morning I reported early for orientation, costume fitting, and makeup tests. Morris had told me to go to the editing building to meet with Rita Clocker, the production assistant and continuity chief. She would give me my schedule.

From the moment I arrived at the compound, the general mood seemed to be panic. When I had worked on a theatrical production before, it was a pretty weird experience. Everyone was stressed about meeting schedules, meeting the budget, and a hundred other crazy details. I could tell from the minute I arrived at Rocky Edge that this production wouldn't be any calmer.

People were running from trailer to trailer, yelling questions back and forth. At first I thought these people were talking about Morris's encounter with the skunk. Maybe they were worried about him, and about what would happen to the production if he got sick from the animal bite.

As I moved closer into the compound, I heard the same questions over and over.

"Does yours work?" several people shouted frantically.

"I have to have one *now*!" a couple of people called out.

I walked toward the editing building, and finally got a clue what the uproar was about. A woman standing in the doorway yelled, "How about notebooks or laptops? Who's got notebooks?"

Suddenly a familiar voice cut through all the panicked strangers. "Nancy! You're here! And you're going to be our Esther."

"Luther," I said. "At last—a calm, familiar voice." I turned to see my friend striding from the writer's trailer.

"I'm right, aren't I?" he asked. "You're going to accept Morris's offer?"

"I am. But what's going on here this morning? Even for filmmakers, this group seems pretty frenzied. And it's only the first day!"

"It's not a pretty picture, is it?" he said as we took in the chaotic scene.

"I heard one of the members of the editing team say something about laptops and notebooks," I told him. "Is something wrong with the editing machines?"

"You might say that," Luther said in his calm, drawn-out way. "Every computer out here has been fried."

3

Stealing Thunder

Fried?" I repeated. "**What** happened?"

"No one knows," Luther answered. "Could be some computer virus. All I heard was that no database, no files, and no software are available to anyone."

"But they must have backup systems," I said.

"They do—and they're also totaled. They can't figure out what's wrong—"

"George can." I didn't mean to interrupt Luther, but the words just poured out. This whole deal sounded suspicious to me. *All* the computers out of commission—even the backups? My antennae were quivering.

"That's right," Luther agreed. "She's pretty good with technology, isn't she?"

"She's a total genius when it comes to computers. I can pretty much guarantee that she'll figure out what's wrong—*and* fix it. Come on, let's find Morris."

It didn't take me long to convince Morris to bring on George. He was really desperate for help. "Believe me," I promised him, "if it's a computer virus, George can snuff it out, and if it's a worm, she can squash it." I decided to keep the last promise to myself: If it's sabotage, she can detect it!

"I don't care what's caused the problem," Morris said, "as long as my computers get fixed." He waved his hands through the air as he talked, and he looked and sounded like he was extremely edgy. "Every aspect of my production depends on those blasted machines," he continued. "Just get her out here as soon as possible!"

"I'll call her right away," I assured him. "We also talked about meeting with the Muskoka Musketeers today. When would be a good time for you?"

"Today?" Morris said, rubbing his forehead. "We've got the table read this afternoon. I don't know . . . with the computers all down . . . I can't schedule anything right now, Nancy. Get back to me later."

I could tell I wasn't going to get anywhere with him. With the computer problem, all the priorities changed. I decided to check in with the Musketeers by myself if necessary. But the first goal was to get George on site.

George not only reported immediately, but she brought three laptops from her own private stock. She's so into computers that she buys or scrounges outdated and half-dead ones to rebuild and reconfigure.

"This is fantastic," Morris exclaimed when George handed him the loaners. "Maybe we can reconstruct some of the lost files on your computers while you're working on our machines. I'll give one to Rita and one to Althea, and keep this one for myself. You're an angel, George! And you are too, Nancy, for bringing her in."

George actually blushed—not something she does very often. But then, she's not called an angel very often either.

"I'm on my way to meet with Rita to get my schedules," I told Morris. "I can take this computer to her, if you like."

"And I can take this one to Althea," Luther said. "We're working through the script today."

"Great," Morris said. "George, you come with me. We've rounded up all the computers for you in the office. Okay, everyone, let's get to work. We're losing time every second—and that means we're losing money."

I headed straight for Rita Clocker's trailer. As I

walked through the compound, I began to understand why Morris was verging on panic. The pace of the compound had now slowed to a crawl. People sat around or stood in groups. No one seemed to be working. A few stretched back in lawn chairs, catching some rays. Others read books, watched battery-operated TVs, or talked on cell phones.

It wasn't until I got to Rita Clocker's trailer that it felt like I was on a movie set again. I could hear her voice through the thin trailer walls as I approached—and she didn't sound like a happy camper.

"Look, people, we're in trouble! I need all of you working at top speed. We have to get this production back on track or you're all out of a job. So move it!"

The trailer door popped open and a young man and young woman burst out and ran off toward different buildings.

I stepped inside the trailer and introduced myself. "I'm looking for Rita Clocker."

"You found her," a woman said without looking up from her desk. I recognized her voice as the loud one that I'd heard as I walked up. She was somewhere in her forties, and was pretty average looking except for a gorgeous mane of dark red hair.

"Nancy Drew, Nancy Drew," she recited. "Oh, yes, you're Esther, aren't you? Let me see . . ." She pawed through stacks of papers until she finally pulled out a small folder. "I suppose you've heard," she said. "Our computers are all shot. So everything's at a standstill right now. A good time for you to get caught up."

She looked me up and down, her eyes sort of squinty, as if she were checking me out. "Mmmmm, I think you'll do nicely as Esther." She scrawled some notes on a torn piece of paper. "You're new to this, aren't you? I think Morris told me that. Your part's really small right now, but it might be expanded. Go get fitted right away for your costumes, and then report to makeup. I'll have a cameraman meet you there, and he can do some testing while they're developing your face colors."

She talked so fast, I had to really focus to catch every word. And she never seemed to actually take a breath.

"Because the computers are all out of whack, I have no idea at this point when we'll be shooting your scenes," she barreled on. "We'll take up the slack time with rehearsals, blocking, and coaching. Lunch is at noon sharp in the mess hall. That's the long metal building over on the bluff. The actors and crew chiefs are doing the table read at two o'clock in the same building. Be there. I'll give you the rest of your schedule then."

She gave me a quick smile, then ducked her head back down to her desk and began studying a clipboard full of charts. I thanked her and headed straight for the wardrobe building.

Rita's rat-a-tat speech was still rattling in my brain, and I found myself hurrying across the compound.

The costume fittings went quickly. They already had some dresses made up, and they just needed to alter them a bit to make them fit perfectly. I usually hate getting fitted for clothes—it's so boring and seems to take forever. But this session turned out to be *very* interesting.

"Wow, did they create that blue cloth just to match your eyes or what?" Tripp Vanilli said when I came out of the dressing room in my first costume. "Honey, you're going to be a great Esther." Tripp was the head designer, and admitted this was only his second film. His assistant, Julie Wilson, had done more movies, but this was her first big-time project.

Julie handed me a long apron to put over the dress. "He's right, you know. This dress isn't exactly evening wear, but it'll be great for the film."

"So how was Rita?" Tripp asked as he pulled some dresses off the rack. "Totally hyper, I bet. She acts like the only reason the computers went down was to inconvenience *her*."

"If you ask me, it's kind of a blessing," Julie said, pinning up my hem.

"Blessing?" I repeated. "How do you mean?"

"This whole production was a mess long before this morning," she answered. "It's probably a good idea for everyone to stop and take a breath."

"But why?" I asked. "Aren't you just getting started? How could it be a mess already?"

"Money, honey," Tripp called over from the cutting board. "Not enough of it."

"This is a budget flick if there ever was one," Julie added. "There wasn't enough money to start with, and some of that's been thrown down the wrong tube."

"Morris seems so sure of himself," I said. "I'm surprised he'd let that happen."

"He's spread pretty thin, trying to be both producer and director," Tripp pointed out. "Sometimes he's so wrapped up in one job, he loses control of the other."

"The sad thing is how it affects all of *us*—the crew and the artisans," Julie said, standing back to check her work. "When we first came on board, everyone was like this great team—a family. We all really believed in the project and were willing to put up with the low budget in order to get the job done and make a really good film. But now . . ."

Her voice trailed off and she just shrugged her shoulders.

"You'll see what we mean," Tripp said. "Everyone's on edge. Our little family has turned into a collection of bickering brats." He brought over a beautiful piece of paisley material and draped it around my shoulders. "Mmmm, nice?" he murmured.

"Absolutely," Julie said. "Okay, Nancy, you're through for now. We'll get right on these, and let you know when we need you for the next fitting."

I thanked them and went over to the makeup trailer.

"Well, now, no mistaking who you're gonna be in this movie, is there?" a cheerful voice greeted me as I stepped inside the trailer. The long room smelled like face cream and hair spray. "Hi, I'm Degas." A short man with broad muscular shoulders and an inky-black ponytail reached up and fluffed my hair. "I'm not going to be doing much here," he said. "You're practically perfect as is."

A woman bustled out of the bathroom and joined us. "You must be Nancy Drew," she said, "our Esther. I'm Pam." She was pretty in a natural kind of way, but it was hard to guess her age. She could have been anywhere from forty to sixty.

"Cosmetician to the stars," Degas added, smiling proudly at his colleague. "You're really lucky, Nancy. Pam has made up some of the most famous faces in the world."

"Have you seen this?" she asked, pointing to a large portrait of a young woman hanging on the wall. It was a blowup of a brownish photograph I'd seen once in the River Heights library. A small sticky note with the word *Blue* had been placed over one eye. Another note stating *Reddish blond* was stuck next to the long wavy hair.

The original photo in the library was old and marred with cracks and spots and smudges. But this version had been cleaned up on the computer, and I immediately saw the resemblance between the young Esther Rackham and me.

"You're definitely that girl, babe," Degas said. "Especially after we get through with you."

"After a couple of hours or so, no one will be able to see the difference," Pam said, gently dabbing my face with globs of a sheer cream.

"If I already look so much like Esther, how come it's going to take that long?"

"That's showbiz, babe," Degas said. "Welcome to the movies."

It took even longer than they'd thought, because they stopped periodically to videotape my head from every possible angle. They made up my face and fashioned my hair for daytime, nighttime, working, barn dancing, and gardening. And they barely stopped talking the entire time.

A lot of the conversation was about people I didn't know or hadn't even heard about. So I steered them in another direction. "I hear this production is having a little trouble getting off the ground," I said.

"*Staying* off the ground, you mean," Degas said. While Pam held the camera, Degas was pinning different hair extensions on my head. I'd just had my hair cut to shoulder length, and Esther's hair was supposed to be about a foot longer.

"This isn't exactly a big-budget production, you know," Degas continued. "We've certainly been there before, right, Pam?"

"Ohhh, yes," she said. She squinted one eye as she looked through the viewer with the other.

"And small films have to cut corners sometimes," Degas said. "We all get that. But this production . . . whoa, it's been a train wreck. One problem after another just eating up the money. And there's just not that much extra to spare."

"But from what I've heard, every film production has problems along the way," I said. "How is this one any different? Some people have said that Morris might not be able to handle producing *and* directing. Do you think that's it?"

"Hey, it's a nutty business to begin with," Degas said. "And you're right—there are always disasters along the way that eat into the budget. But this one *is* different somehow—and I don't think it's really Morris's fault, do you, Pam?"

"No, I don't," she agreed, putting down the camera.

She looked over at the portrait of Esther Rackham. "The things that happen . . . well, they just don't seem to be accidents, that's all. It's like this whole production is jinxed. Reminds me of a picture I worked on thirty years ago. No one ever figured out who—or what—was causing all the problems. Some even thought the ghost of the main character was kicking up the trouble . . . didn't want her story to be told. Finally had to close the whole production down for good . . ."

Pam's voice just sort of faded off as she ended her sentence. I glanced over at Degas. He raised one eyebrow and pursed his lips as he looked back at me, but he didn't say anything.

By the time the two of them had finished with me, my head had been pulled, plastered, and peeled, dabbed, jabbed, and scrubbed—at least a dozen times. Amazingly, when I finally left the trailer, my face felt soft and tingly.

I was also hungry, and late for lunch, so I headed straight for the mess hall. It was one of those metal temporary buildings assembled on the grounds just for providing food to the actors, crew, and staff.

"Wow, you look different somehow," George said when I joined her at a long table. "Your eyes are all made up," she said, "and that's actually a cool lipstick shade. Bess would be proud."

"I wish she were here to see it for herself, before it gets eaten off with my sandwich. How's it going with the data recovery?"

"It's going to take time," George said, sipping a soda. "Whatever happened to those machines, it was a thorough destruction."

"A computer virus, maybe?"

"Maybe. I should know more by the end of the day. At least I brought a couple more laptops from my own stock that they can use this afternoon."

We had to eat quickly, because the table read was scheduled for two o'clock, and it was already one thirty. But between bites I managed to tell George about my sessions with the wardrobe and makeup teams.

When we finished eating, George and I joined the others who were assembling at the end of the room. George handed over the two laptops, and then left to go back to work on the production company's machines.

The rest of us took seats around a large table. Morris sat at the end of the table. His assistant and Rita Clocker were on his left, and Althea Waters and Luther sat on his right." This is always one of my favorite days when I'm filming a movie," Morris said, "the first time I get you all in the same room at the same time. Some of you already know each other, but let's go around the table anyway and introduce our-selves. I'll start," he said with a wide grin. "This is the table read for the movie *Stealing Thunder,* and I'm Morris Dunnowitz, producer/director."

His words were accompanied by the muted *clack-clack* of his assistant's fingers flying over the keyboard of one of George's computers.

"Althea, you're next," Morris said.

"Hi, everyone, I'm Althea Waters, the scriptwriter. You all know what the movie is about. I call it *Stealing Thunder* because it's about stealing money from the sale of anvils, and in Greek mythology, the Cyclops made thunder by beating on anvils."

Luther beamed with a broad smile and nodded as she spoke. I could tell he liked her.

One by one we all introduced ourselves. The directing, production, filming, and recording crew chiefs were all there, as well as the entire cast. I jotted notes in my pocket-size, black-leather notebook as each person spoke.

"As most of you know, I'm Herman Houseman." The man who was speaking was very handsome—fiftyish—with thick brown hair and a deep voice that carried all through the room. "I will be playing the hero of this story, Mr. Ethan Mahoney, an early settler of this quaint town who made a killing manufactur-ing anvils. And whose fortune would have been much more substantial were it not for those nasty fellows."

Mr. Houseman swiveled in his chair and shot a mock glare across the table toward the two men sitting to my right.

"Hold on there, Ethan," the one next to me said with a gorgeous grin. "We were just doing our jobs. Hi, everybody. I'm Luke Alvarez, and I play John Rackham." He stopped to nod toward the guy on his other side. "And this is my brother in real life, Ben, who plays my screen brother, Ross."

"Hey, all," Ben said, with an equally sparkling smile. The Alvarez brothers were young and *really* good looking. Although they both had thick shocks of dark wavy hair and enormous brown-black eyes, they weren't twins, and each had his own distinct charm. I was sure I'd seen them in small roles on television dramas.

After everyone was introduced, the table read began. I quickly learned that a table read is just what it sounds like. All the actors read their parts aloud from beginning to end. Morris read the scene setups and the action, and the others followed along in their own copies of the script. Althea had done a good job of telling the story in an exciting way, and all the actors seemed to enjoy reading through their parts.

Most of my scenes were with Ben and Luke. According to the legend, when a steamer full of money came down the Muskoka to buy some of Ethan's anvils, the Rackham brothers successfully ripped it off and were never heard from again. Although she tried, Esther failed to stop them, and she went to her grave without ever revealing their whereabouts. As we read our parts, the brothers and I seemed to get into a groove right away. It helped me shake off my initial nervousness.

When we got to the end of the script, everyone was quiet for a moment. Then we spontaneously burst into applause. It was sort of like the cheers that sports teams give themselves before the big game.

"Okay, everyone, that's it for today. Take the evening off—tomorrow we start shooting. Make sure you know when you're required, and where. Rita has all that info. Thanks for a great read."

"Well, now, this is going to be fun, don't you think?" Ben asked me as we stood. "I haven't seen you before. Have you worked in television? Film?"

"Ummm, no, nothing like that. I'm a real beginner at this—and a local resident, actually."

"No kidding," Luke said. "Well, Morris said to take the evening off. For us, that means fun on the town. How about being our tour guide?"

"Yeah," Ben agreed. "How about it, Sis?"

"Nancy!" George's voice interrupted me before I could answer Ben and Luke. I turned to follow the sound of her voice. She was standing in the doorway and motioning to me to join her.

"Give me a few minutes, guys," I told the Alvarez brothers. "I need to talk to my friend."

"Hurry back," Luke said, smiling and waving at George. "She's more than welcome too."

I walked to the doorway to join George. "What's up?" I asked her.

"Come on, you've got to hear this," she said. She led me outside the building to a clearing near the edge of the bluff. As we walked, I began to hear voices—loud and angry.

"All the excuses in the world won't let you off the hook this time," I heard Rita Clocker say. Her voice was easy to recognize.

"I'm not making excuses," a man's voice yelled. "I'm telling you that it *can't* be done—not on this timetable! You and Morris have been way off base from the beginning on this schedule. You've got to give us more time to get that boat ready, or you're going to have a disaster on your hands."

"You know the pressure we're under here," Rita fired back. "If you were the least bit professional or had even an ounce of pride in your work, you'd do everything you could to get the job done."

When George and I reached the clearing, I recognized the man arguing with Rita. He was the chief carpenter on the production, and he was waving a piece of paper in Rita's face.

"They've been going at it for about twenty minutes," George whispered.

"We *are* doing everything we can!" the man roared, his face purple with rage. "But obviously that's not good enough. Lots of luck with this shoot—you're going to need it!"

Then he wadded up the paper and lobbed it at Rita's nose.

4

Lights!

Rita ducked as the wadded paper flew toward her face. The chief carpenter strode across the clearing without looking back.

As Rita watched him walk away, she looked as if she was going to explode. She scooped up the wadded paper and sailed it off the bluff. Turning back around, she seemed to notice George and me for the first time.

She looked a little embarrassed, and frankly, I felt uneasy myself at being caught just standing there and watching. I decided to offer my help and hurried over to her. "Rita, I'm sorry," I told her. "We heard your voices. Is there anything I can do?"

"Can you hammer a nail?" she replied with a lop-sided smile. "Looks like our carpenter chief walked off the job."

She started walking back to the mess hall, and I fell into step beside her. George followed. "What happens now?" I asked. "Can you just move someone up from the current crew?"

"Not really," she said, quickening her pace. "There are strict rules covering all the tradesmen on a film. The head carpenter has to fit certain criteria and have specific certification. I don't think anyone else on the team has all the credentials. It'll take days to find someone on the coast and get him flown out here. I just can't believe this!"

Rita found Morris inside talking to Luther. She interrupted their conversation and vented all her frustration and anger in one long sentence. When she finally stopped talking, she took a huge gasp of air, then plopped down into a chair.

"Any chance we can get him back?" he asked her.

"I don't think so," she said. "Besides, I don't think we want him back. He hasn't been doing the job, and he's got a major attitude problem."

Morris rattled off the names of some people he knew in Hollywood that might serve as replacements. But he agreed that it would be hard to find one that was between assignments and available to begin immediately. "I can't deal with any more delays," he said, running his hand through his hair.

"Does it have to be someone from Hollywood?" I

asked. I glanced at George and smiled. She smiled back, and I could tell she'd read my mind.

"Okay, Nancy," he said, "you've been my chief local headhunter so far. I need someone who can take over carpentry management—at least for a while, until I can get someone in from the coast. I can't pay much, because the budget's strained to the edge right now. But the new guy will get his name in the credits, and my undying gratitude. And if he does a good job, he'll have a glowing recommendation that I guarantee will get him steady work in the business."

"How about if it's not a guy?" I asked. "My friend Bess Marvin is an ace carpenter. She's built stage sets for local productions. She's worked her way through certification and trade licensing. And she would *love* to work on this film."

"Plus, she'll charm the rest of the crew into doing exactly what she says," Luther added.

"Call her," Morris said. "I might still have to bring in someone from the studio to head up the crew, but it sounds like she'll be great until then. I definitely need another person hammering nails, at the very least. We're pretty close to shutting down for today," he said, checking the round gold watch he carried in his pocket. "Have her report tomorrow, if she can."

"I'm not sure we'll be able to hold her off until then," I said. And I was right. I called Bess right away, and it took her about half a second to yell, *"Yes!"* And within forty minutes she was at the compound.

"We did it!" she called out, as she ran from the parking lot to greet George and me. "I knew it was a good idea to get my licensing and trade certification last summer. Now here we all are—part of the crew working on a real Hollywood movie!"

"A *television* movie," George reminded her.

"I know," Bess said, "but it's still a real movie—a major production."

"A shoestring production," I corrected her. "This is a low-budget project. And Morris is not the big-time Hollywood director/producer Luther thought he was."

"Okay," Bess said with a huge sigh. "Low-budget production, television movie. I get it. But at least we're working on it—and Nancy's even acting in it. Come on, you two. We have to start somewhere!"

"True," I conceded. There was never any point in trying to hold off Bess's enthusiasm. It was like a tornado. You just got swept up in it.

"You're right," George said to her cousin. "It *is* cool, and we are definitely going to have fun."

"Wait till you meet the Alvarez boys," I added. "Come to think of it, what happened to them? I was supposed to be their tour guide for a night on the town in River Heights. They must have left without me."

"So, how about a tour of a movie production camp instead," Bess said. "Come on, I want to see everything! Where's my shop?" she asked, looking around. The sun was already down, and although the worklights were still on, the whole compound was beginning to be overrun with dark shadows whose shapes shimmered and morphed as we watched.

"Okay, it's tour time," George announced. "Come on, Bess. We'll show you around."

We walked through the middle of the compound. George and I took turns pointing out the different trailers and temporary buildings, telling Bess about the specialized activities that each one housed. Then we strolled around the fringe of the compound. At one end, we showed her the carpentry building.

"Do people actually live in their trailers while they're here?" Bess asked.

"Some do," George answered. "Some have hotel rooms in town."

"And some do both," I added. "Stay out here part of the time, but still keep a room in town if they need to get away from it for a while."

"So this is where I'll be hanging out," Bess said. She wandered through the carpentry section, inspecting tools and looking over plans. She quickly changed from excited movie fan to pro carpenter. "I can do this," she said, nodding.

"I never doubted it for a minute," I said. "Come on, let's continue your tour."

George and I took Bess into the sound studio. None of the interior sets was finished yet, but we could see the beginnings of what would be the Mahoney Anvil company office and the boat that carried the money for the anvils.

"Looks like I've got a lot of work to do," Bess murmured, looking around. "None of these sets is anywhere near ready for filming."

"Listen to her," George said. "She's taking charge already. They're shooting some scenes at exterior locations too," George said. "Right, Nancy?"

"Right," I answered. "They're using that old abandoned cabin out in Humphrey's Woods for the Rackham brothers' place. And I'm not sure where they're shooting the river scenes. The last I heard, they were even thinking of shooting them on Swain Lake."

"Instead of the river?" Bess said.

"Yeah, maybe," I answered. "Luther said it has something to do with insurance or property rights—he wasn't sure. The only exterior locations that are confirmed are the cabin and the one for the scene in which the mountain lion attacks Ethan Mahoney just as he's about to catch up to the Rackham Gang."

"Shouldn't that all have been decided by now?"

George asked. "It seems kind of late in the game to be scrounging for locations."

"Not for this production apparently," I said. "Come on, let's go find some dessert in the kitchen, if it's open."

We walked toward the mess hall. It was really getting dark now. There was no moon. The interior yard of the compound was well-lit by large worklamps mounted high on columns. But behind and between the buildings and trailers, the night was inky black.

"If they're so intent on cutting corners and saving money, I'm surprised they're including the scene about Ethan and the mountain lion," George said. "What are they using for the lion? Mrs. Cartwright's golden retriever?"

"Oh, no," I replied. "We have an actual menagerie in the camp! Follow me."

I took them around the last trailer, which was labeled WRANGLER. "That's Jake Brigham's trailer. His animal friends are out back." I led them to a stable, but the door was locked.

"Hey, girls," a friendly voice said. "How ya' doin'?"

"Jake . . . hi," I said. He really looked like a wrangler—leather hat with a floppy brim pulled down over thick silver hair, golden tan, muddy boots.

"Here to say hi to the horses, are you?" he asked. "'Bout time you all met."

"Sure," I answered. I introduced him to Bess and George, and then he unlocked the stable door. Inside were four horses, two roans and two palominos. A black cat had carved out a comfy bed on a worn blanket lying on a stack of hay. The horses looked a little uneasy.

"Whoa," Jake murmured. "Whoa, now. This is Esther—she's going to be your friend for a while." He turned to me. "Come on over, Nancy. Make friends."

I moved slowly from horse to horse, stroking their faces and talking to them while Jake introduced me.

"Nancy's going to be riding with these babies," Jake told Bess and George. "In the film, Ross Rackham drives the wagon to the river, John is in the back, and Esther rides on the seat next to Ross. You ever ride in a horse-drawn wagon, Nancy?"

"Only once," I answered, "in a parade through town. I even drove the horses, but the trainer was on the seat beside me, just in case."

"My gals here are very tame," Jake said. "These two are the stars," he added, pointing to the first two, "and those are the stand-ins. We'll have a few more in here by the time we start shooting. The Alvarez brothers will be riding their own horses too."

"Is there really going to be a mountain lion in the movie?" Bess asked. "I remember the one from the legend."

"That's right, missy," Jake said, crouching down to act out the scene. "Just about the time Ethan Mahoney's catching up to the Rackham boys, a mountain lion plunges from the woods and attacks him." He brushed off his jeans and smiled. "We're usin' a stunt double for Mahoney in that scene, of course. Can't have Herman Houseman bein' menaced by a wild animal."

"So do you train the lion, too?" George asked.

"I do," he answered. "Would you all like to meet them? They're out back here."

We all answered with an enthusiastic yes, and he led us out of the stable. After locking the door, he took us to a large trailer parked about thirty yards away. "Even though we're all friends," he explained, "it still spooks the horses a little when they hear the lions whining, so I park their house over here."

He punched a complicated combination into the lock on the door of the huge rig. Then he asked us to wait outside while he checked in with his charges.

Finally he opened the door and ushered us inside. The front of the rig was filled with standard mobile-home type decor—built-in furniture, a loft for extra sleeping. But halfway back, a heavy-duty cage wall divided the room into two medium-size ones. Inside, two beautiful cougars lounged on plush cots in their own rooms. They were the color of caffe latte, and they wrinkled their noses high in the air when we approached.

"Kaia . . . Thunder . . . these are our friends," Jake said to the cats in a soft voice. "Be nice."

One of the lions yawned, and the other reached around to wash her shoulder with a long undulating tongue. The yawner then walked to the front of the cage and rubbed his cheek against the metal. I could hear him purring like a chainsaw as Jake went over to scratch the creamy-tan head.

"They're so beautiful," Bess whispered.

"Kaia is the star," Jake told us. She looked the part, grooming herself on the cot. "Thunder here is her stand-in. I raised their mom, and I've had these two since they were born. They're my buddies, right, fella?"

Thunder's purr echoed around the room. "We'd best go now," Jake said. "My stars here need their beauty sleep." He pushed some treats into their cages, and then ushered us out of the rig. He took us around to the back of the trailer, where he had connected a large cage. "I take them out here every day for exercise and training," he said.

I thanked Jake for the tour, and Bess, George, and I walked back to the main part of the compound. I took Bess over to Rita's trailer so she could check in, but there was no one there. Then we went to the mess hall. It was late, but the chef was puttering around in the cozy coffee bar in the back corner.

Over coffee and brownies, I told Bess and George about the rumors I'd heard from the wardrobe and makeup crews. Then I asked George about the disabled computers.

"It was a thorough job," she said. "Every machine in the place was shot."

"This production seems to be having a lot of trouble getting off the ground. We've had an attack skunk, a computer outage, and one of the top tradesmen just walked out. Is this all just bad luck? Or is someone trying to stop this movie before it even gets started?" I asked.

"So we have the same old questions we always have with a mystery," Bess said. "Who would do such a thing? And why? I'm glad I'm on the payroll now. I'll keep my eyes and ears open."

"Me too," George said. "I should have more information for you tomorrow, Nancy. But I just don't get what anyone would have to gain by sabotaging *this* film. It isn't exactly a Hollywood blockbuster. Why would anyone want this movie squelched?"

George thought for a moment. "Maybe it's the Rackham brothers," she mused. "They don't want anyone to know the true story ... so they're haunting the compound!"

We were all quiet for a few minutes, each of us in her own thoughts as we sipped our coffee. Then a chilling murmur echoed around the metal walls.

"Whooooooooooooo," a voice moaned from the shadows across the room. "Go awaaaaaaaay. Don't tell our storrrrrrrry."

I couldn't help it—I jumped. We all did. It was so dark in the mess hall except for our corner. But after the initial shock, I knew who it was.

"Okay, guys, you're busted," I called to the shadows. "Come on out."

Luke and Ben Alvarez strolled over to join us. "We almost gave up waiting for our tour of River Heights," Ben said. "I'm glad we found you. And the more the merrier," he added, smiling at George and grabbing the seat next to her.

"Ben and Luke Alvarez, these are my friends George Fayne and Bess Marvin," I said. "George is getting the computers back on line, and Bess is filling in for the carpenter chief who walked out."

"Hel-*lo*," Luke said, putting his coffee down and pulling his chair closer to Bess. "We haven't met, but that doesn't really matter, does it?" He rested his chin on his hand and flashed a dazzling movie star grin.

"Does that line usually work for you?" she asked with a friendly smile.

"Sometimes," he said. "How about this one: I have

a little beach house back home. I like to sit on the deck and look at the ocean on a cloudy day. And your eyes are the exact color of the water."

"That's *definitely* better," Bess said with a special sparkle in her blue eyes.

"So are we going to hit the River Heights nightlife, or what?" Ben asked.

"It's pretty late," Bess said, "and I have to report in really early tomorrow. Maybe we could take a rain check, and try for—"

Crrrrrrk! Zzzzzzzzzzp! Sssssssssspt!

Weird noises interrupted Bess, and the lights in the coffee bar flickered.

"What's going on?" the chef yelled from the kitchen. "My stove is crackling."

"It's not just in here," I called back, hurrying to the window. "The security lights outside are flickering too."

Ominous pops and crackles resounded in the mess hall, and the lights dimmed down to blackness. One by one, like dominos falling, the lights in the kitchen sparked one by one, and went out. A whirring noise purred through the air, then grew louder.

"What's happening, Nancy?" Bess asked.

"I don't know, but I think we should take cover. And stay away from the lights." We raced away from the mess hall to a sheltered spot behind the office trailer. As I peered around our refuge, I saw a large bolt of blue lightning leap between the security lights, blanking out each one as it hit. For an instant it was dead quiet. With a sizzle and a whoosh of air, everything went black.

5

Camera!

"I smell fire!" George yelled. "It's the soundstage—the soundstage is on fire!"

"It might be the generator—it's in a semi behind the soundstage," I said, dialing 911 on my cell.

George, Bess, the Alvarez brothers, and I joined the others who were still in the compound and ran to the soundstage building. Jane Brandon and a couple of men toted fire extinguishers. It looked like I had guessed right—scary noises popped and crackled from inside the semi behind the soundstage.

As we got closer to the truck, my nose filled with that prickly smell of an electrical fire. Several people were trying to get inside the semi, but the huge doors on the side of the rig were padlocked. As we heard the fire engine sirens approaching, Jane fumbled with the padlocked door, and the extinguishers shot a circle of foam on the ground around the semi.

The rest of us kept a safe distance while the chemical retardant burst out of the hoses. The amateur fire crew was able to contain the fire until the pros arrived. I recognized River Heights Fire Chief Cody Cloud leading the pack. They didn't even try to fiddle with the padlock. They pulled Jane and the others out of the way, and then tore into the truck with axes and put out the fire.

While the others cleaned up, Chief Cloud looked around. He recognized me and waved. "Nancy!" he called, walking over. "This isn't the first time you've beaten me to a fire. Is anyone hurt?"

"I don't think so," I told him. "There aren't that many people on the grounds right now. The director gave most of us the evening off."

"You working here now?"

"She's in the movie!" Bess declared.

"I see," he replied. He was clearly not impressed. "Well, wait right here," he added. "I want to ask you a few questions." He left to talk to a couple of the people who had been the first on the scene.

Meanwhile Jane and another man came over to talk to us, followed by Luther and Morris. Jane introduced the man with her as Dave Linn, the other on-site security officer. We were telling him what we'd seen and heard when Morris and Luther ran up to join us.

"What happened?" Morris asked. "We were at the cabin getting ready for tomorrow's shoot. Is everyone all right?"

"Seem to be no injuries," Dave said. "But we've got a mess on our hands. When that generator blew, it caught fire. The rig was locked, so the firemen used axes to break into the truck and get to the fire."

"The generator!" Morris exclaimed. "It's practically brand new! How could that happen?"

"That was my question," the fire chief said, rejoining us. "I've got some men checking over the site now. We'll stay with it until we get some answers."

"It was an accident, though," Morris prompted. "It was an accident, right?"

"That's what we're going to find out, sir," the fire chief said. "I've got my top arson investigators on it. Pretty odd, it blowing up like that. No rainstorm tonight, so lightning didn't hit it. Hard to figure some sort of spontaneous combustion event. Don't worry—we'll get to the bottom of it. I'm on my way back there now to talk to my men. I'll be checking in with you later."

The fire chief left, and Morris turned to the rest of us. "Okay, what happened? Nancy, were you here?" he asked. "Did you see what happened?"

I repeated what I'd told the fire chief. "I saw no one suspicious," I concluded. "I didn't hear any vehicles start up or drive away from the scene. Of course, it was pretty chaotic right then, with people running to the soundstage and yelling for help. But I didn't see or hear anything that didn't fit. Except . . ."

I turned to Jane, who was jotting my words in her notebook. "Jane, I watched you try to unlock the semi, but there was something wrong. Did you have the right key? What was the problem?"

"I had the right key, but it wouldn't work," she explained. "I tried the other keys, but none of them fit the lock either."

"We need to check that lock," I told her. "Either it was jimmied, or maybe it was a different padlock." I turned to Morris. "We might need to check purchase orders to see whether it was the original lock, or if someone substituted a new one."

"I don't remember buying a new lock for that door," Morris said. "And believe me, I've been checking every purchase we've made around here. At this point, I can't even *afford* a new lock."

"Are you thinking that this wasn't an accident, and whoever sabotaged the generator used a new padlock to close it up?" Bess asked.

"Exactly," I answered. "Either they broke the original one, and had to replace it so the break-in wouldn't be discovered before the generator blew out, or they used a different padlock just to make it impossible to get inside without causing further damage and more trouble."

"I don't believe we've met," Morris said to Bess. "Are you part of Nancy's investigative team?"

"Sometimes," Bess said with a grin. "I'm Bess Marvin."

"Your new carpenter," I added. "Sorry about not getting around to introducing you two. Bess, this is our boss, Morris Dunnowitz."

"Welcome aboard, Bess," he said. "You've got a lot of work ahead of you, but Nancy says you can handle it."

"Jane, we need that padlock as soon as you can pry it away from Chief Cody," I said.

"No problem," she said. "I'll go keep an eye on it now."

"So you don't think this was an accident at all, right, Nancy?" Morris asked. "What do you think happened—and who do you think did it?"

"I don't have any idea," I answered. "Right now, all my suspicions are based on nothing but a hunch."

"A hunch based on experience," Luther pointed out.

"I think it's pretty weird that the generator blew," I said, "especially in view of the other problems you've been having around here. George, was the generator connected to any of the production company computers?"

"Yes, a couple of them—they're keyed in to the generator chip, and programmed so that the electricity usage coordinates with the production company schedule. But those were the first ones I got back into service. A manual override was used while the computers were down, but we switched back to electronic management when I restored those machines."

"Could someone have played with the data, and programmed the generator blowout?" I asked.

"Maybe," George answered. "I can check that out."

"What about the Muskoka Musketeers?" Dave suggested. "I saw their protest camp along the road when I drove up here. They waved all sorts of signs about how the production company is upsetting the natural balance of the riverbank in this area."

"I don't know," Luther said. "They're a pretty quiet bunch. They've never done anything really destructive. It's kind of a leap from hiding a skunk in a closet—if they did that—to blowing up all the power for the production company."

"Luther's right," I added. "We need to cast the net a little wider. And we might be way off base anyway—we don't even know for sure that the generator blowout wasn't just a horrible accident."

I didn't really believe that it was for a minute. I was

just trying to keep Morris's hopes up a little longer. But it didn't take long to clear up the question. The fire chief reported back, saying that the blowout was deliberately engineered.

Morris slumped against a tree. "We're sunk," he said in a low voice. "We can't shoot a film without electricity. We can't finish the sets, we can't go on location to the cabin or the river, we can't even feed the crew. I haven't got the budget to replace the generator—I doubt if I can even afford to try to fix this one. We've got a couple of small backup generators to get us through minor problems, but it's not nearly enough to run the whole production."

"Would you like Bess to take a look?" I suggested. Bess nodded eagerly. "She's just as good with motors as she is with hammers and saws."

"Let me scope it out," Bess urged. "Maybe I can work out a sort of parasite setup, so that the big one feeds off the two backups. At least we might be able to nurse them along for a while, until you can come up with a better plan."

"If we don't get the electricity working, we won't need you to fill in as carpenter," Morris told Bess. "We won't need anybody out here at all, because the production will shut down. Please look at the generator and see if there's any hope. And I'll even pay you the industry rate. It might have to be in installments, though."

"Whatever," Bess said. "If I don't get it all at once, I won't spend it all at once."

"No one's going near the scene until we're through with our investigation," the fire chief warned. "Then you'll have a real cleanup ahead of you before you can do any patching or start up the machines. I'd say you're looking at tomorrow afternoon at the earliest."

"Okay," Morris said. "It's too late to alert all the crew now. Everyone reports to breakfast at nine. Rita and I will work on the schedule tonight. Maybe we can figure out a way to take one of the small generators to the cabin tomorrow for a location shoot while Bess works on the other two back here."

"And George will check out the computers involved and see if there's anything suspicious going on there," I said.

Luther checked his watch. "Well, I'm late for my date," he said, "so I'll be leaving you all now."

I looked at him and smiled. "With Althea?" I asked.

"Yes, with Althea," he said, with a mock frown. "It's a *work* date." Then the fake frown faded, and he grinned back at me.

"What about you, Nancy?" Morris asked. "What's your next move?"

"I'm going to talk to the fire investigators first. Then I might stop off at the Musketeer camp on the way home."

"Nancy, what would we do without you, Luther, George, and Bess?" Morris said. "You've brought us the only good luck this production has had. Thanks so much. Okay then, everybody, we all have our assignments. See you tomorrow."

Luther left to meet with Althea. Morris and George went back to the office, and Bess and I walked to the generator semi. The electric-burn smell still filled the air.

We stepped around glops of fire extinguisher foam and puddles of muddy water. A wide step stool had been placed in front of the semi. I saw Chief Cody standing just inside the rig, talking to one of his investigators. When he saw Bess and me, he hurried down the step stool.

"Now, Nancy, I know why you're here," he said, "but we don't have anything for you yet. I told you I'd get back to you as soon as I knew anything."

"Can you just tell me whether it was an accident or not?" I asked him.

"No, I can't tell you that yet," he answered firmly.

"Okay. How about letting us inside, just for a minute or two. Bess is going to be repairing this machine, if possible, and she wants to see how big that job is going to be."

He shook his head, but then surprised us by saying yes. "All right," he said, "but just for a few minutes. Watch where you step and stay out of the way. If you find something suspicious, call one of us over—don't touch it yourself."

I hurried over to the step stool before he could change his mind. Bess followed closely.

"Boy, Chief Cody wasn't kidding when he said it was a mess," Bess muttered. The fire crew had placed a few large-beam lanterns around the inside of the rig, so it was pretty bright in there. And it was humid. Water dripped and trickled from the walls and slicked up the thick, carpetlike padding on the floor.

Only two people were inside there with us—a man was videotaping the whole interior, and a woman stood beside the generator. It was a huge, multiunit machine. Bess gasped when she saw it.

The investigator was systematically panning across the surface of the blackened machine with a special light. I recognized the instrument she was using as a multiple-color-band forensic light source. It was sort of like a UV black light, only much more precise. Forensic investigators use it to pick up traces of blood and other evidence that can't be seen by the eye alone.

"Have you found anything yet?" I asked her. I tried to sound casual, as if I were just another investigator asking an official question. It worked. She answered without even looking up.

"Not on the machine," she answered. "Just the blood drops on the floor. I probably won't find any on the generator," she admitted. "If there was any, they would have been blown off by the hoses. But the stuff on the floor . . . it seeped down into that pad."

She finished her inspection while Bess and I cautiously looked around. Finally the woman left to join the investigator at the other end of the semi.

"This thing is huge," Bess said, inspecting the generator. "It will take me forever to patch it up." She took time to look it over and jotted a few notes on a pad. "That's about all I can do right now," she finally said. "Without being able to touch it or try to start it up, I'm just guessing about whether it's even possible to fix it."

"Come on, you two," Chief Cloud called from outside the rig. "You've been in there long enough. Let my team do their job."

He helped us descend the step stool. "How soon can Bess get in here to really inspect the generator?" I asked him. "You heard how desperate the director is to get the electricity back up and working."

"I fully understand the seriousness of the situation," Chief Cloud said, firmly steering us away from the rig. "And I will inform Mr. Dunnowitz when it's okay to let people back in the semi."

I thanked him, and Bess and I walked to our cars. "Looks like George has already left," Bess said, checking her watch. "Her car is gone. Are you still going to stop by the protest camp? It's pretty late."

"I'll check it out when I drive by, and decide then. Let's ride in together tomorrow. Morris said everyone will be at breakfast here at nine."

"I'll drive," Bess volunteered. "And I want to get here early. The sooner I get into that generator, the sooner this movie will get back into production. I'll pick you up at seven." She got in her car and started it up. "I'll follow along with you. If you stop at the camp, I will too."

I drove out onto the road, with Bess following closely. The Muskoka Musketeers' encampment was pretty dark and looked closed down for the night, so I decided to wait until the next day to talk to the protestors. I waved a "forward" gesture to Bess. The two of us had an uneventful ride back to River Heights.

Bess and George picked me up at seven on Monday morning in Bess's car. Bess had already told her cousin about our peek inside the generator rig.

George passed out samples of muffins and juice from one of her mother's catering experiments and shared what she'd learned from the computers. "The generator hookup is really protected," she told us. "Password, full encryption, and—best of all—a tracking system. It's set up so that anyone entering the program leaves a marker that can be traced back to that person."

"So did anyone hack into the program?" I asked.

"I'm still working on it," George said. "But I'll find out. It takes a hacker to find a hacker."

When we arrived at the compound, hardly anyone else was there yet. We went straight to the mess hall where the caterers were setting up a breakfast buffet.

Bess was thrilled to learn that she could get into the generator semi. She took the keys from Morris, promising to let him know as soon as she could give him an estimated timetable for recovering power. We went back to her car to get her huge tool cart and headed for the semi, dragging the cart on its four wheels.

The axed-out hole in the side of the rig had been boarded up. We climbed the step stool, and Bess unlocked the doors and slid one open. Everything looked the same inside except for the addition of good lighting. Someone had installed six battery-operated spotlights on tall stands. We switched them all on, and the long room was flooded with light.

We wrestled the tool cart up into the rig, and Bess began puttering with the generator. I inspected the rest of the room, jotting notes and taking pictures. But I didn't find anything that could be called a clue. I wasn't surprised—a lot of people had trooped around in there since the generator blew out, and Chief Cody's investigators seemed to be pretty thorough.

Bess and I were so absorbed in our separate investigations that we both jumped when Rita Clocker's voice blared through a bullhorn: "Will everyone on the grounds report to the mess hall, please. Company meeting right now in the mess hall."

"Yikes, it's nine twenty already," Bess said. "Morris wanted us all there at nine sharp." She put her tools away in the cart, closed it up, and locked it. I dropped my notebook and camera into my backpack, and we scurried out of the semi. Bess locked the rig, and zipped the keys in her cargo pocket.

When we got to the mess hall, most of the cast and crew were there. George waved us over to her table, which seated eight. Luther and Althea were already there, and Luther introduced Bess to Althea.

"Somebody sitting there?" Bess said, nodding to the seat next to hers. That place and the one next to it were littered with empty muffin and butter wrappers, wadded-up napkins, and used forks.

"Luke and Ben," George answered. "They went back for seconds. I haven't even had firsts yet— Mom's muffins were enough breakfast for me."

"And almost enough for me," I agreed. "But I think I'll get some more juice. How about you, Bess?"

"Juice would be good," she answered. "I'll come with you."

By the time we got back, Morris had arrived in the hall and was barreling toward our table. He pulled Bess and me aside so we could talk privately. "What do you think, Bess?" he asked. "Do you have any idea when we can get back up to speed?"

"It'll take me a few more hours to patch the big generator, but then not long to hook it to the other two. You should be back on schedule by midafternoon. I just don't know how long the parasite system will last."

"Oh, that's great!" Morris said. He seemed not to have heard her last sentence. "Can I use one of the small generators this morning?"

"Sure," she said. "I won't be needing it till afternoon. He grabbed her in a big hug, then bolted off to the small stage in the corner of the room.

"Looks like most everyone is here," he said into the bullhorn. "And I can tell by the buzz I heard around the compound this morning that most of you already know what I'm about to say." He talked for a few minutes about the generator blowout, praising the quick response of the security team.

"One of the local mechanical geniuses is helping us out," he continued, smiling at Bess, "so we hope to be back to full power soon. Meanwhile, I'm changing the schedule slightly. It's nine forty-five now."

A huge belch exploded from my left, and several people at the nearby tables giggled. "Oops, sorry," Luke murmured with a sheepish smile. "Shouldn't have had that second plate, I guess." He ducked his head down and burped again into his napkin.

"At eleven we'll rehearse scene twenty-one at the Rackham cabin in the woods. I need all cast and crew for that scene to report to the shuttles in one hour. Don't be late, guys. We want to do some light takes with the noon sun." He started to leave the little stage, but paused for a moment, looking down at someone sitting at the table in front.

"Hey, are you feeling all right? You don't look so . . ." His words trailed off, then burst through the bullhorn again. "We need help up here!" he yelled, jumping off the stage. I stood up.

"Someone's having a heart attack!" Morris yelled. "Medic!"

I started toward the front of the hall. I'm certified in CPR, and I knew I might need to put some of that training to use. People around the room began jumping up and crowding around the area where Morris stood. George tapped 911 into her cell phone.

I'd only gone a couple of yards when I heard Bess's voice behind me. "Nancy! Wait," she called. "It's Luther!"

I suddenly understood what people meant when they said they "stopped cold." When I heard Bess's voice, I felt a chill rattle down my back. I rushed back to the table. Luther was doubled over in his chair and his face had turned a pale greenish gray. With a grinding groan, he dropped off the chair onto his knees. Then he crumpled to the floor.

6

Cut!

"**L**uther!" I knelt beside him. His face was still an ashy color, but his eyes were open. "My stomach," he moaned. "Terrible cramp . . . Really hurts."

"Get one of the medics over here," I told George. "He needs help right away."

As George raced off to find one of the on-site medical staffers, I heard another groan nearby. Luke Alvarez tumbled to the floor, overturning his chair with a metallic clang.

"Nancy, there's something awful going on," Bess said. "Lots of people are getting sick. A few are even unconscious."

"It looks like food poisoning," I told her. "Check on Luke, will you? Just try to keep him comfortable. If he's chilled, throw a jacket or a tablecloth over him.

Don't give him anything to eat or drink—not even water."

Near the entrance Morris and his security team were working with the company doctor and nurse to set up triage. They grouped all those who had become ill so that when the ambulances arrived, the sickest people would be treated first.

For the second time in two days, I heard emergency vehicle sirens driving into the compound. Within minutes George returned with one of the emergency medical technicians—EMTs—who'd arrived in an ambulance. I left Bess with the EMT to care for Luke and Luther, and asked George to come with me. We headed first for the kitchen. Grabbing bags of small plastic cups and lids, we went back out to the serving tables and the breakfast buffet.

"We need two sets of samples from everything," I told George. "Everything on the buffet: eggs, sausage, yogurt, waffles, cream cheese, burritos, fruit, protein smoothies—even the bagels and sweet rolls, the syrup and salsa, the mustard and the water. We need a set for the paramedics, and I want one set for me."

I knew it would be important to have the samples so that doctors could determine just what type of food poisoning everyone had contracted. It would also help determine what medicines and treatments to use.

We worked quickly, spooning samples into the cups and labeling them. Then we snapped on the lids and dropped the cups into two bags. By the time we'd finished, the most seriously ill—including Luther and Luke—had been taken by ambulance to hospitals in the area. Others were being taken by shuttles, and some were evaluated on site and released, with suggestions to see their own doctors for possible treatment.

"What's going on, Nancy?" George asked when we had finished giving all the samples to the EMTs. "Was this just bad food, or are we looking at more sabotage here?"

"We're going to find out soon, I hope," I answered. "That's why I'm getting my own samples. One set's for the doctors, one's for the criminal investigators."

"So your instincts are telling you this was intentional."

"My instincts are telling me to not take anything for granted, and to consider this a crime until I find out the truth. If this poisoning was intentional, whoever is doing this has crossed the line."

"I fired the caterers," Morris said, joining us as we watched the last vehicles leave for town. The three of us took seats at one of the tables. "They said they weren't to blame, but I can't take any chances. It's hard enough to get insurance for this production as it is."

"I agree," I said. "Even if they were supercareful with their refrigeration and preparation, it looks like something—or someone—got to the food. So that means they weren't careful enough about keeping everything clean, or their security wasn't tight enough."

Morris sighed and nodded. "I see you're thinking the same thing I am. It was no accident." He didn't wait for a response. "Nancy, we have to get this figured out. The doctors have shut me down for at least a couple of days. It'll take that long for the sickest people to get completely well—and that includes some of the stars of the film. Jane says it will also take that long to finish the security investigation. She said there's an outside chance it wasn't the food."

"You mean it might be another kind of infection?"

"Yes, maybe bacteria in the ventilating system or the water, or some virus carried by insects."

Neither of us mentioned the other possibility— sabotage by the same person or people who damaged all the computers in the compound, and snuffed out all the electricity.

"Do we have to evacuate the compound?" George asked.

"No, the investigators say they can work around us," Morris answered.

"The best bet is food poisoning, and they should be able to find out if that's what this is very quickly,"

I pointed out. "Then the investigation turns immediately from *what* to *who*."

"Well, shutting down this production for two days is a financial disaster," Morris said. "But I'm not giving up yet. I'm going to spend that time trying to raise more money. If I don't get it, the shutdown might be permanent."

"I should have all the computers online by tomorrow," George promised. "And Bess said she'd have the generators hitched together before then."

"That's true," Bess said, walking up. "Maybe sooner. Boy, this food poisoning was awful, wasn't it? I'm so glad we didn't eat any breakfast."

"Me too," Morris said. "I'd been so busy working out the new schedule with Rita, I hadn't eaten yet either. I had planned on loading up a plate after I'd finished with the announcements. We were lucky."

"Now that you fired the caterers, what are you going to do about food up here?" George asked.

"I hadn't even thought about it yet," Morris said.

"I work with my mother," George said. "She's the best caterer in River Heights. And she's never poisoned her customers," she added with a crooked smile. "I'll check with her if you want."

"That would be great," Morris said. "It's just one less thing I have to worry about. If she's got the time to take us on, have her get the details from Rita." He stood up. "Thanks again for all your help, girls. Keep me posted." His shoulders were slumped as he walked out. I wondered how much more he could handle before he gave up.

"What about the Musketeers?" Bess asked me. "Do you think they'd be capable of some of the stuff that's been going on? Other than the hidden skunk, of course."

"Luther thinks they're pretty low-key types," I answered. "Not the kind of ruthless people who'd actually put someone in the hospital with food poisoning. But I still want to talk with them. I was originally scheduled to rehearse with Jake and the horses for part of this afternoon. If that's still on, I'll probably stop by the Musketeers' camp later, or on the way in tomorrow morning."

I looked at my watch. "It's a little after noon. I've got just enough time to run these food samples in to the lab before my session with Jake. Let's check back with one another here around four."

"Sounds good," George said. "I'm pretty close to breaking through the last electronic wall into the company computers. I might have news to report by then."

"I should have the generators humming by then too," Bess said.

Bess and George went off to their tasks, and I went to mine. I drove Bess's car back to River Heights and the chemistry lab at the university, where a friend of mine was an assistant professor. I'd helped him with a case a few months earlier, so I knew he'd be happy to return the favor. I dumped all the food samples off with him, and he promised to begin checking them right away.

When I got back to the movie compound, I reported to the menagerie. I spent a couple of hours working with Jake. He showed me how to ride on the bouncy seat of a buckboard without looking ridiculous. He also let me take the reins a couple of times for an exciting run along the bluff trail.

After scheduling another session for the next day, I checked in with the security team. Both Jane and Dave were there.

"Hi, Nancy." Jane greeted me with a warm smile. "What have you got for us?"

"I was hoping you had something for *me*," I answered. "Have you heard anything from the fire investigators? Do they know whether the generator blowout was an accident or not?"

"We're pretty certain it wasn't," Jane said. "My key didn't work in the padlock because it wasn't the original lock. The company had not bought a new one, so we think it was put on there by the trespasser."

"To cover up the fact that someone had been inside," I guessed. "Anyone who glanced at the door and saw the padlock would assume everything was okay."

"The new lock is very similar to the old one," Dave added. "We compared advertising-brochure photos. But it's a pretty common lock—it'd be hard to trace it to its point of purchase."

"Apparently the first lock was cut open," Jane said. "We found shavings of metal matching the original lock on the ground beneath the doors. We also found traces of blood there."

"There was blood inside the semi, too, in the padding near the generator," I pointed out.

"That's right," Dave said. He seemed surprised. "So we could be looking for someone who already had an injury—or someone who scraped or cut their hand or finger while they were cutting the lock open."

"And it has to be an inside job," I said, "by someone who knew the location of the generator and when it would be deserted."

"Someone who didn't have a key to the lock," Jane continued. "We have one here, the maintenance crew has one, and Morris has one somewhere."

"He couldn't locate it this morning, though," Dave pointed out.

"The culprit had time to plan everything very carefully," I continued, "which meant getting a backup padlock similar to the original. Have you noticed whether anyone in the cast or crew has a fresh wound, aside from Morris's skunk bite?"

"Jake Brigham has a half dozen new wounds a day," Dave said. "Animal bites, scrapes and cuts from leashes and reins, punctures from bird talons."

"One of the carpenters stabbed his palm with a nail building the boat set," Jane offered. "Rita sliced her finger with a drafting knife when she was making the new schedule board. Lee Chang pinched his wrist tightening a camera he'd mounted on a cherry picker. And Althea broke her nail grabbing her laptop when it started to fall. She saved the computer, but tore half her nail off in the process."

"I guess the question is, is there anyone in the company who *couldn't* have bled on the generator," I said. "This seems to be a company of the walking wounded."

"In more ways than one," Jane said.

We talked a little about scheduling a good time for a visit to the Muskoka Musketeers' protest camp, and I left.

At four fifteen I walked to the mess hall. A yellow crime tape was strung across the door, barring anyone from going in. Next door George's mother had set up a tent to use until the original mess hall was cleared for food preparation again. Bess was waiting for me there.

"George said to go ahead and eat," she told me. "She'll be here later."

Mrs. Fayne's food was not only safer than the previous caterer's, it was much better. Over burgers and fries, Bess and I caught up.

"I've got good news," Bess said. "We'll have full power in about an hour. I'm waiting for a part that's being constructed in the metal shop."

"Great job!" I told her.

"I'm looking forward to getting started on the carpentry. There's a lot of lost time to make up."

"Plus it's more fun working with a shop crew than being all by yourself in that semi, I'll bet."

"It is," she said. Then she put down her burger. "You know, there's a lot more work to do than just set building. Nancy, the morale is pretty low. I found that out when I was in the metal shop working on a generator part. More of the craftsman are talking about walking out."

"Because of the problems getting the film off the ground?" I guessed.

"Yes, but Morris is part of it too. Some of the crew think that he might be in over his head, and that's made him a little desperate."

"And they think *he's* causing the problems?"

"Well, one of the rumors I've heard is that he's gotten so far over budget already—without any footage even shot yet—that he's in a lot of trouble personally. Some people think he's being forced to sabotage his own production as a way of getting out of the project without destroying his reputation in the industry."

"I'm not sure I believe that," I told Bess. "But I've been fooled before." I made it a rule long ago to follow every lead, no matter how strange it seems. "Sounds like it's time to talk to Morris."

Just then my cell phone rang. It was my friend at the Riverview lab. We talked for a few moments, then I closed my phone.

"It was definitely food poisoning," I reported to Bess. "Salmonella. No way to tell whether it was intentional, of course, but he said there was enough to make a small army really sick. We're lucky there weren't more people stricken."

"Right," Bess agreed. "And speaking of food, I have a message to pass on. Harold Safer is looking for you."

Mr. Safer loves the theater and show business. "I'm surprised it took him this long to get out here. What did he want?"

"He brought a sample platter for Aunt Louise's catering, but I saw him hanging around Herman Houseman's trailer. I don't think his main goal is selling cheese."

"Come to think of it, Mr. Houseman made his

name on Broadway. I know he's gotten at least a couple of Tony Awards. That's enough to send Mr. Safer totally into orbit. Why did he want to see me?"

"Nancy, you're not just one of the workers out here. You're in the *cast*—one of the actual actors! He probably figures you're his best bet for an introduction to Herman Houseman."

"You're probably right. I'll keep an eye out for him."

When we finished eating, I packed up some of George's favorite cookies and walked to the security trailer. I told Jane and Dave about my chemist's report, and left the cookies. Then I headed for the office. I could hear Morris yelling inside as I approached the door.

"Who do you think you are?" he said, "walking in here, telling me how to run my business!"

"Do you think no one has heard about the problems you've been having out here?" I heard another man say. The voice was familiar, but I couldn't place it right away. "Protest demonstrations, generator blowups, food poisoning outbreaks—and worst of all, a script full of lies and distortion! This production has become a loose cannon—and it's aimed right at River Heights."

"We've had some problems, sure," Morris responded. "But I've spent nearly a year planning this film, and it's going to be as historically accurate as I can make it. Nothing you can say will ever change my mind about that."

"Don't be so sure of yourself. There are laws against slander," the other voice continued. "You're treading a fine line between portraying history and ruining the name of my family and the name of my corporation."

When I heard that, I realized who the other man was. When I opened the door, I was face-to-face with Jack M. Halloran, distant relative of the Rackhams and CEO of Rackham Industries. He didn't even seem to see me. Anger blazed from his eyes, and he wheeled back around to face Morris.

"Shut down this production," he warned. "Or I will!"

7

Stunt Double

"Come on, Jack," Morris said. He had dropped his
angry tone and sounded now like he was talking to
an old friend. "You don't mean that. You know we're
trying to do the best job possible on this film—to
make it not only exciting, but accurate. We're not out
to sensationalize your family's history. I thought we
had an understanding."

"Yeah? Well, understand this: Pack up and get
out—or this will be your last production." Jack Halloran spun around again, and for the first time, he
seemed to notice me standing in the office doorway.
He's a big man; he looks as if he could swing a few
anvils around himself. And just then he looked *very*
angry as well.

"Mr. Halloran, hello," I said quietly. He seemed startled to hear my voice as he aimed his glare right into my eyes. "I'm Nancy Drew, remember? I haven't seen you since—"

Then he seemed to look through me. Without a word, he stormed toward the door. I stepped out of the way just in time to allow him to pass by.

Morris watched Halloran stomp off. Then he glanced over at me, and looked away quickly. His face was hard to read, but he looked as if he was hiding something. Was it embarrassment? Or anger? Guilt, maybe? I couldn't tell. Whatever it was, it looked like he didn't want to face me.

Finally I broke the silence. "Morris? What was all that about? Do you know Jack Halloran?"

"Not really," he said. "I met him a couple of times when we first started talking about this project. He seemed totally on board with it then and offered his support. Seems to have changed his mind, wouldn't you say?"

"It sure sounds like it. What brought this on, do you suppose?"

"He said he got a copy of the screenplay in the mail, and that it completely distorts the truth about the robbery and about his family."

"Well, since the truth is that his ancestors did in

fact pull off the biggest heist in this state's history, I'm not sure what he's upset about. I know Althea's script is accurate. Luther's seeing to that."

"I told him he was way off base, and that there was nothing in the script that attacked his family from a personal standpoint. But he's adamant about shutting us down."

"Did he show you the script he got? I wonder if he got the final version."

"No, I didn't see it," Morris answered. "You don't suppose he's behind some of the problems we've been having around here? He's got a lot of money—that can buy a lot of sabotage."

"I don't know—he has a pretty good reputation, Morris. He seems to be an upright guy—he's on all the right boards, sponsors some major charities, and runs a corporation full of loyal employees."

"Yeah, a lot of people are like that until you start digging up the past." Morris got this strange expression again. Was he finally reaching his limit? He looked as if the prospect of a major fight with Jack Halloran was going to be the final blow.

"If you need to talk to someone local about any legal—"

"No, thanks, Nancy." He cut me off before I could say any more. When he turned, his expression was still a mystery. "I have to get to a finance meeting," he said, looking at his watch. He definitely wanted me out of there.

"Sure, no problem," I answered. "But, remember—"

"Thanks," he said. He clipped the word off so fast, I barely heard the *s*.

I could tell he wasn't in any mood to talk about production problems, so I smiled, wished him good luck, and left.

As I walked along the path, I went over the confrontation between Morris and Halloran in my mind. Halloran was right about most of it, of course. There had definitely been problems with the production from the very beginning. But that business about the script—that made no sense at all.

Morris was right too. Halloran certainly had the technical expertise and resources—and the money—to pull off all the sabotage. If he was determined to stop the making of *Stealing Thunder,* he could do it—one way or another.

As I walked I heard a sputter, and the huge worklamps scattered around the compound began coming back to life, even though it was still light out. "Bess, you rock!" I whispered.

I stopped by Mrs. Fayne's catering tent for a latte, and found Harold Safer there, talking with her about his cheese samples.

"Nancy! I've been looking *everywhere* for you,"

Mr. Safer announced. Sometimes his speech is very dramatic.

"Mr. Safer. Bess told me you were here."

"Is this one of the most exciting things that has ever happened to River Heights, or what?" Harold said. "A movie . . . being made right here . . . and *you're* the star!"

"Now, Mr. Safer, you know better than that. You know the Rackham Heist legend as well as I do. Esther played a pretty small role then, and I'm playing a pretty small role now."

"But you're *in* the movie, Nancy. You're actually acting with one of the giants of the Broadway stage."

"Herman Houseman."

"Yes," Mr. Safer said. "I saw him in *Long Day's Journey into Night* six years ago. It was a triumph." As I watched him describe the event, I noticed something remarkable.

"Mr. Safer," I blurted out, interrupting his story. "Do you realize that you *look* like Herman Houseman?"

"Me? Oh, don't say that," Mr. Safer protested. "He's so handsome, with such a classic profile and dramatic eyes."

"Just like you," I insisted. "No kidding, you could be his double—his stand-in."

"Oh, no," Mr. Safer said. "Never. I could *never* presume to fill his shoes." I could tell that the idea appealed to him, in spite of his denials. "Still," he continued. "I'd surely love to meet him, to actually shake his hand—to tell him of my admiration for his marvelous talent." He paused, waiting for my response.

"Sure, Mr. Safer," I agreed. "Come on, let's see if he's around right now."

Mr. Safer took off his chef's apron—the one that modestly declared HAROLD SAFER, CHEESE MERCHANT in Old English script. Then he washed his hands, combed his hair, and proclaimed that he was ready.

We walked to Mr. Houseman's trailer. It had the best location in the compound, on the bluff, with a beautiful view of the Muskoka and the meadows and forests beyond, leading to the horizon. Painted on his door was his name and a gold star.

Harold took a deep breath as we approached, and released it in small whistling puffs.

I knocked several times, but there was no answer. I thought I saw a curtain move slightly, so I called out. "Herman? It's Nancy Drew. Are you in there?"

There was still no response, not even another curtain flutter.

"I'm sorry, Mr. Safer, I guess he's not here right now. He could be in a dozen places—coaching, wardrobe, memorizing lines, rehearsing. He wouldn't want to be interrupted in any of those, I'm sure. Can you come back up tomorrow? I'll track him down for you then."

"Of course," Mr. Safer said. "I really need to get back to town anyway." I saw how disappointed he was, and I was determined to get him an introduction. He walked back to Mrs. Fayne's catering tent, and I strolled over to the generator semi. It was locked, so I went to the shop and found Bess there.

"I was just going to look for you," she said. "Has Harold Safer found you yet? He was bugging me again about talking to you."

I told her about my conversation with him.

"Are you sure Mr. Houseman wasn't hiding in the trailer and just not answering you?" Bess asked. "He doesn't seem very friendly to me. He's definitely got an attitude."

"Well, I'll wear him down—for Mr. Safer's sake. Is the generator fixed?"

"It is. When the sun goes down tonight, we'll have lights—at least for a while. I closed shop for dinner, but some of the crew will be back this evening for another shift. And they'll have power, at last."

"So are you coming back in, too? I'm looking for a ride home. I have a coaching session tomorrow, and then a major rehearsal with the Rackham boys. And I don't know all my lines yet. I have to get those down before then. I'm taking the evening off so I can show up prepared. If you're planning to stay for the evening,

I might be able to catch Mr. Safer before he leaves."

"Actually, I was planning to go home for a shower and change of clothes at least. I've been working in that damp old semi nearly all day. I might come back later, but I can take you now if you're ready. I talked to George a little while ago. She ran into another glitch, and intends to stay all night, if necessary, so she can finish the computer recovery by tomorrow."

We stopped by the catering tent to leave a message for George with her mother. Then Bess drove me back to River Heights.

"What about the Musketeers?" she asked as we zipped past their protest camp.

"I definitely want to talk to them, although I agree with Luther that they're probably not behind the really serious problems with *Stealing Thunder*. Check back with me later this evening. If I'm comfortable with my lines by then, we can finally talk to the Musketeers on the way in to work tomorrow."

"Sounds like a plan."

We spent the rest of the ride to town talking about the case. I told her about my conversation with Jane Brandon, and our speculations about the padlock and blood at the generator semi. Then I relayed the exchange I'd overheard between Morris and Jack Halloran.

"Halloran," Bess murmured. "He probably makes more money in a week than Morris's budget for the whole movie!"

On Tuesday morning Bess picked me up, and we drove straight to the Muskoka Musketeers' protest camp. George had stayed up most of the previous night, but had finished the data recovery. She had agreed to spend the next several days dividing her time between computer technical support and helping her mother with the catering.

The Musketeers' camp was pretty rustic: makeshift shelters mixed with weathered, well-used hiking tarps and fresh-out-of-the-box family-size pup tents.

"Hi, I'm Bongo," a friendly young man said as we got out of the car. "Are you here to join the cause?"

"Not exactly," I answered. "I just wanted to ask you all a few questions."

"You're reporters? Great," he said. "Hey, everyone, come on over. We're getting some publicity at last!"

I saw no reason to dispute his claim. I took my notebook and pen from my jeans pocket. I could tell from Bess's smile that she would play along.

"So, you're saying that the moviemaking company is disturbing the environment, is that right?" I began.

"Sure, man," Bongo said. "You got big semis tearing up all these little country roads. Machine shops, carpentry shops, food preparation. It's like they're putting in a little village up on that bluff. You can't do that. What about all the waste and sewage? Where's all that supposed to go up there?"

"Well, I assumed the company has waste disposal plans in place, don't they?" I suggested. "Some sort of operation that either recycles or gathers up waste to be deposited in the city dump, maybe?"

"Do they have a plan?" Bongo asked. "That's all we want to know. What are they doing to protect the environment while they're there? And what do they intend to do to restore it to its original state when they leave?"

"Right," several Musketeers shouted.

"And what about the wildlife?" Bongo continued. "How about all the creatures who've been living there undisturbed for centuries? How do they handle all the disruption? What steps are being taken to protect the wildlife?"

"Speaking of that," I said, "we hear you used a skunk to make a point about your protest. I'm not sure capturing a skunk, locking him in closet, and leaving him to whatever fate he gets when he's discovered is the best example of protecting the wildlife."

"Okay, okay, that might seem a little harsh," Bongo

admitted. "But sometimes there have to be sacrifices in order to gain a larger victory."

"There have been other incidents in the compound," I said.

"Yeah, we've heard about some of 'em," Bongo said. Some of the others around him nodded, and some smiled. "Computers whacked up, generator blitzed." He frowned at me. "Hey, you're not implying—"

"She's not implying anything," Bess interrupted with one of her winning smiles. "We're just trying to get all the story."

"We're not really into destructive behavior," Bongo said. "We prefer our messages to have a little whimsy." He smiled proudly. As he talked on about his cause, I dutifully took a few notes. Finally, I cut him off.

"Well, thank you," I said. "I believe I have enough for my story."

"Say, which outfit are you with?" he asked, following us to Bess's car. "You with print or broadcast?"

"I'm a freelancer," I told him, climbing into the passenger seat. "I'll let you know when I sell the story."

"Mm-hmmm, you do that," he said, closing my door. "Nice car, by the way." Bess started the ignition. "Hey, we're not the only local residents who are fighting this movie. Do you know they've got a couple of mountain lions up on that bluff? We haven't had mountain lions around River Heights for fifty years," he called out, as Bess backed up to turn around.

"Talk to some of the farmers in the area," Bongo continued. "See how happy *they* are about someone reintroducing a mountain lion into the neighborhood."

I was a little late when I finally arrived at the coaching trailer. The dialogue coach, Donnalee Collins, was waiting for me, but she didn't say anything about my being late. She was entertaining Jake Brigham, the animal wrangler, with stories about her years on Broadway.

Donnalee looked familiar to me as soon as I saw her. There were some posters and still shots on her trailer wall, and I recognized her as the host of a long-running series on the History Channel.

First she showed me how to use an old-fashioned way of speaking so that it sounded natural and not fake. We worked with a mirror, so I could see how my face muscles moved to form certain sounds. Then she taped me as I ran some of my lines, so I could actually hear my speech the way it sounds to everyone else.

Jake had brought the canary that would play Muriel, Esther Rackham's pet bird. The canary was trained to do its part, but it was time to coach me in mine. During one of the scenes, I was supposed to let Muriel perch on my finger, while I fed her tidbits with the other hand.

I'd been around pet birds before, although I'd never had one of my own. But I'd never actually fed one by hand, and there's sort of a trick to it. I had to learn how to feed the bird just the right amount of food and hold it just the right way. That meant neither I nor Muriel would let the scene get sloppy by dropping the food. It also meant not having the bird mistake my finger for a tidbit.

As Muriel and I worked, Jake and Donnalee guided us both through our paces. When Ben Alvarez arrived, I was ready to rehearse the scene, with him playing Esther's brother Ross Rackham.

"How's Luke?" I asked him, as Jake and Donnalee moved the furniture around to set up the scene. "Is he still in the hospital?"

"No, he came back to the hotel last night," Ben answered. "But he was still looking pretty green. He said he felt a lot better this morning. I trust we get a rain check on that tour of River Heights nightlife?"

"Absolutely," I assured him. "Just let me know when Luke is ready to party."

The run-throughs went really well, and I was so glad I'd taken the time the night before to get my lines down perfectly. We had a half-hour break before the next rehearsal, so I checked in with Jane and Dave to tell them about my interview with the Muskoka Musketeers. They agreed with me that the chances were pretty slim that the Musketeers could pull off some of the major sabotage that had taken place.

Then I met up with Ben and Jake at the menagerie, and we rehearsed the buckboard scene again—this time with Ben driving instead of Jake. We worked for a couple of hours, and the last few times went pretty well. But I had a feeling it wouldn't be the last time we rehearsed that scene. We also made the rounds in the wagon a few extra times, while I held the reins.

By five thirty even Jake had had enough, and he declared the rehearsal over. Ben and I wandered over to the catering tent for some food. "George!" Ben called out when he saw her bringing a tray of fruit to the buffet table. "You're working here now? Is there no end to your talents—a computer genius *and* a marvel in the kitchen? Marry me—marry me *now*!" Then he clasped his hands over his heart and dropped to one knee.

"On your feet, Romeo," George said with a laugh. "I'm way too busy to get married right now. Get back to me in about ten years, and we'll talk."

"Wounded!" Ben cried in a booming voice. "Wounded to the quick by the young maiden with eyes the color of bittersweet chocolate. Bittersweet indeed." He slumped into his chair.

"Enough," George groaned. But she raised one eyebrow and flashed him one of her best smiles.

After we ate, we packed a box with a sandwich and juice for Bess, and lattes and biscotti for all four of us. Then we pulled Bess away from the shop long enough for an impromptu picnic and dessert at the edge of the bluff. While we watched the sunset, Bess and I told Ben and George about our encounter with the Muskoka Musketeers.

By the time I left the compound that evening, both Bess and I felt really wiped out. My body ached from bouncing on the buckboard and handling the reins of the horses. Although I was eager for a hot shower and my warm bed, Bess and I made a quick stop at the hospital on the way home to check on Luther.

Althea was visiting him when we arrived. Luther looked and felt a lot better, and told us he'd be back to work the next day. They were happy to hear I had finally interviewed the Muskoka Musketeers. But they were both surprised to learn about Morris's verbal bout with Jack Halloran.

"I can't imagine what version of the screenplay made Halloran so angry," Althea said.

"Did you send him a copy of the script?" I asked her.

"No, I'd never do that," she answered. "I wouldn't want it floating around out there. It upsets me just to think about it."

"I'm going to contact him about it," I assured her.

"Well, at first it was tempting to think this movie

was merely jinxed," Luther said, with a half smile. "That maybe Althea's attempt to bring this dark story to the screen had aroused the angry ghosts of the Rackham brothers. But it's pretty clear that this production is being sabotaged by more human hands—although, I agree, probably not the earnest hands of the Musketeers."

"Do you think maybe the Rackham ghosts are expressing themselves through their descendent Jack Halloran?" Althea offered.

"That's hard for me to believe," Luther said, "but not impossible."

"Well, the whole thing is impossible for me to believe," Bess said with an exasperated sigh. "This is a practically-no-budget film—"

"With a cast of beginners and amateurs," Luther added, "scripted—"

"By an unknown writer," Althea cut in.

"So what earthly motive would anyone have for shutting it down?" Bess concluded.

"Nancy, I believe that's your cue," Luther said. All three gazed at me with expectant looks.

"Ummmm, I'll get back to you on that," I told them. "Looks like it's time to kick this investigation into high gear."

When Bess and I left, Luther and Althea were head-to-head over the latest script revision.

· · · ·

Wednesday morning most of the cast and crew were back after the two-day hiatus. The food poisoning outbreak had taken its toll emotionally as well as physically. Morale seemed to be at a new low, in spite of Bess's and George's victories on the mechanical and electronic fronts, and the superior quality of Mrs. Fayne's food service.

I reported to the soundstage, where Morris had planned to shoot some trial footage of one of the cabin interior scenes. This included not only the bird scene I'd rehearsed the day before with Ben, but also the next scene, in which Luke arrives after hearing about the shipment of money.

This was the first time I'd seen Morris since our exchange after his fight with Jack Halloran. He still seemed rattled and preoccupied, although he was his usual friendly self to the actors and crew.

The first part of the scene went pretty well. We rehearsed a couple of times, and then he shot a half dozen takes. Next was the scene where Muriel, the canary, sits on my finger while I hand-feed it.

"Let's go straight to camera," Morris said. "No rehearsal. We don't want the bird to be stuffed by the time we shoot." Everyone chuckled, and that helped me lose some of my nervousness.

"Okay, quiet everyone. I want absolu[te] we don't want to startle Muriel. If you can[not] quiet, leave the set." He waited a few minutes to allo[w] anyone to leave that wanted to.

"All right," he said in a low voice. "This will be Take One. Nancy, are you ready?" I nodded. "Lee?" Morris checked with his cinematographer. "All right, then, Nancy. . . . Action!"

I walked to the corner of the "room." The birdcage hung from a high stand and was covered in a pale muslin. Carefully I pulled the cage cover open. I was suddenly engulfed in an attack of nerves. I could feel everyone in the room watching me. I fought to keep my breathing normal, although I felt like panting in order to get enough air.

I pulled the cloth away to show the canary sitting on its swing. I couldn't seem to stop my hand from trembling, and my thumb bumped the cage. That started a chain reaction. The cage began to jiggle, and then the swing jostled.

Muriel keeled over backward and landed on the floor of the cage with a soft thud.

r-the-Shoulder Shot

C ut!" Morris yelled.

At first I didn't move. Seeing Muriel fall stiff onto the cage floor was such a shock, I felt bolted to my spot. Then a communal gasp from the dozen or so spectators jolted me out of my stupor. I realized I'd been holding my breath, and took in a huge gulp.

Suddenly I realized that all was not what it seemed. First of all the cage door was hanging open. Secondly the heap on the cage floor didn't look like the bird I'd been rehearsing with in Donnalee's trailer.

Cautiously I reached into the cage and touched the lifeless bird. Then I pulled it out and held it up for everyone to see.

"It's a fake," I told them, "a toy bird. It's not Muriel."

Several people rushed over to confirm what I'd discovered. "Well, where *is* she?" Rita asked Jake when I deposited the artificial bird in her palm. "Where's Muriel?"

"I don't know," Jake said. "She was in there when I covered up the cage. Rita, you checked the cage when we put it in the corner. You saw her."

"I saw her *then*," Rita said. "But I'm not seeing her now. She's gone!"

"Gone!" Morris repeated. "Where?"

"How would I know?" Rita answered. She sounded frustrated and hassled. "Where does any bird go when it flies the coop? Up in a tree somewhere, I imagine." She looked into the woods that bordered the bluff. Without powerful binoculars, there was no way any of us was going to spot that small yellow bird in that thick stand of trees.

"Jake!" Morris yelled. "Where's Jake?"

"Right here." Jake Brigham strode across the set. His face was crinkled into a mass of worry wrinkles.

To anyone who didn't know much about moviemaking, it would have seemed like this was no big deal. It was just a bird in a very short scene—and all it had to do was eat. But it really *was* a big deal. I found that out in the coaching session. Muriel was not just any yellow bird—she was a trained canary. She'd been taught not to be distracted by sudden noises and bright lights, for example, and not to be startled by people walking around and shouting instructions.

"So, where is she?" Morris asked. "Where's my Muriel?"

"I'll find her," Jake said. "I'm sure she'll fly back on her own soon. Something spooked her, or she'd never have left. Someone must have released her, and chased her off."

"And tell me again how that could have happened?" Morris said. He wasn't yelling anymore, so I inched closer. I didn't want to miss anything. "How could someone have even gotten into the animal area?" Morris demanded. "Where were you? Where were your assistants?"

"Look, I understand why you're upset," Jake said. He'd lowered his voice too. They were both trying to have this totally private conversation in the middle of a large group of people. "I'm telling you, I'll get her back," Jake insisted. His face was getting really red. Morris had asked some good questions. Nothing should be more secure than the animal wrangler's area. If someone could break into that, there wasn't one area of the entire location that was safe from troublemakers.

"What are they saying?" I heard George's familiar

whisper from behind. "Does Jake have a clue about what's going on?"

"Nope," I murmured. I told her what the two men had said.

"But how could anyone break into the wrangler's area?" George asked, echoing my thoughts. "It's supposed to be totally off limits."

"And really secure," I pointed out. "I doubt that it was an accident."

"I assume you've got a backup for me," Morris said to Jake. "A stand-in canary." His lips were drawn tight across his teeth as he talked, and he looked like a volcano about to erupt. George stepped up next to me—we were riveted to the action in front of us. It was almost like watching a movie.

"Yes, but you know as well as I do that it's going to take a little time to get this bird up to speed," Jake told Morris. "I'll need to work with Nancy—the stand-in canary has to get used to her. I'll do some run-throughs with the two of them."

"How long?" Rita asked. "How long before we're ready to shoot?"

"A couple of hours, I guess," Jake answered.

"More lost time," Morris said. "We've already lost *days* of shooting. Now the actors are ready, the lights, the cinematographers. The whole crew is keyed into this one scene. And you're telling me we all just stand around for two hours and wait?"

"Look," Rita said to Morris. "We can't lose any more time. It'll take us hours just to scrap this shoot and set up for another one. Nancy and the boys are here, and they're ready to go. Let's just skip the bird bit and shoot without it."

"No." Althea Waters hurried up. "You can't leave out the bird. We talked about this," she said to Morris. "Remember what Luther said. The bird is really important to Esther's story line."

Morris shook his head at Althea. For a moment it looked like he was going to agree with Rita.

"I'm sure you've already spent a ton of money just getting those birds all the way out here in the first place." Althea kept talking, her words rushing out as she pleaded her case. "And you're paying Luther for his expertise. You might as well get your money's worth from all of them."

"And Nancy's really good. I'm sure she'll be able to switch to the new canary without any trouble," Jake added.

"All right, all right," Morris said with a huge sigh. "Break, everyone—but stand by. When Rita calls, I want you all back here in seconds!"

"Nancy, I haven't totally been on board with your idea of sabotage up until now," George said. "But I'm beginning to be a believer. There's no way we could have *this* much bad luck."

"Exactly," I agreed. "And I'm beginning to narrow the field of suspects—"

"Come on, Nancy, let's go." Jake was motioning to me to get to work.

"Tell Bess what's happened," I told George as I headed toward Jake. "Let's get together later. I want to run some ideas by you two."

As I walked with Jake to the menagerie, I was in sort of a daze. I could hear Jake rattling on beside me as he told me about the new stand-in canary, but I couldn't stop thinking about the problems plaguing this small production.

The new canary was as well trained as the original one—and I was well trained by then too. My rehearsals with the new bird went quickly, and Jake and I reported back to the set with the new Muriel in an hour and a half.

We shot half a dozen takes before Morris announced lunch. Bess, George, the Alvarez brothers, and I found a table for six and tore into plates of Mrs. Fayne's excellent lasagna. About halfway through the meal, I heard a familiar voice.

"Might I join you all?" Harold Safer asked.

"Sure, Mr. Safer, have a seat," Bess urged. She introduced him to Ben and Luke. "This lasagna is so good because Aunt Louise uses Mr. Safer's mozzarella and Italian sausage," she said warmly. Bess is wonderful at putting everyone at ease.

"So how did the shoot go this morning?" Mr. Safer asked me. "I hear you were working on one of the cabin interior scenes."

"That's right," I said. I wasn't at all surprised to hear that he knew the specifics. As much as he loved the theater, being on the set of a film in production must have been heaven for him—and he was probably hanging on every word he heard.

"And you're going down to the cabin itself on location this afternoon, is that right?" he asked.

"Right," Ben answered. "That's when Nancy and I take a ride on the bucking buckboard. I tell you, I'd rather ride a bronco without a saddle—its back is bound to be softer than that wooden seat!" I nodded an agreement as I sipped some water.

"So is Mr. Houseman on the grounds?" Harold asked me. He tried to make his tone casual, but I could see he was extremely interested in my answer.

"As a matter of fact, I think I see him over there. Come on, Mr. Safer."

"Really? Are you sure it will be all right?"

"Of course, come on."

We both wiped marinara sauce from the corners

of our mouths. Mr. Safer took a huge gulp of cranberry juice, and I led him across the room.

I stopped at a table with a RESERVED card perched in the middle. Around it sat Morris, Rita, Lee Chang, Donnalee Collins, Althea, Luther, and Herman Houseman.

"I'd like you all to meet my friend Harold Safer," I said, pushing him forward just a little. He's a River Heights merchant and is supplying the cheese and sausages for Mrs. Fayne's food service—including the ingredients for your lasagna today," I added, taking a page from Bess's etiquette book.

I went around the table, introducing each of them. Everyone greeted Harold warmly, and a few made special comments about his delicious contribution to the meal.

"And this is—," I began, as I got to the person I'd saved for last.

"No introduction is needed, Nancy," Harold said. "Mr. Houseman, you're my biggest fan. I mean, I'm *your* biggest fan. I've seen every Broadway and off-Broadway production you've done in the last twenty years, including your most recent *Long Day's Journey*. Masterful, absolutely masterful."

Mr. Houseman wiped his hands on his napkin with a few large swipes, then stood almost at attention, facing Harold. "My dear Mr. Safer, you honor me with your words. It is always a special pleasure to meet someone with a genuine love of great theater." He held out his hand.

Harold wiped his own palm against his trousers and clasped Mr. Houseman's in a firm handshake.

"I hadn't realized this before," Luther said. "Harold, you could be Herman's stand-in. You're both the same height and build; you have the same profile and hair."

"I told him the same thing," I said.

"I'm very honored by the comparison," Mr. Safer said, stepping back a few inches.

"If we didn't already have an understudy, I'd hire you," Morris added. "Nancy's spontaneous employment agency has already bailed us out of several jams so far!"

"Well, we won't keep you any longer," Mr. Safer said, backing away a little more. "Please continue your meals. It was lovely meeting you all."

"Oh, Nancy, that was wonderful," Mr. Safer said in a soft voice as we returned to our table. "If I can ever do you a favor, you only need to ask."

After lunch the Alvarez brothers and I joined the crew and Morris on location at the abandoned cabin in Humphrey's Woods. I didn't have any dialogue in this scene. According to the script, the Rackham brothers were returning to their home. They get off their horses and have a long conversation about their intentions and don't realize I'm in the garden beside the cabin, hearing every word.

Morris spent hours setting the scene and shooting dozens of takes. Then—just when I thought we were through—he set up the cameras for the reverses. Reverses show the same scene, only from the opposite angle. In this scene, that meant we first had to shoot the whole thing dozens of times from Ross Rackham's point of view.

Next all the lights and cameras were repositioned so we could shoot the scene dozens of times from John Rackham's point of view. Later, in the editing room, Morris and his editor would cut and splice the scene the exact way they wanted, switching the points of view to make it realistic.

Finally we heard Morris call out the magic words: "Okay, everyone, that's a wrap for today." If we all hadn't been so tired, we would have cheered. Instead, we just started filing to the shuttles that would take us back up to the compound.

We had walked only a few yards when we heard Morris shout again. "What?" he yelled. "How could that happen! Hold it, everybody. Come on back!"

We dragged ourselves back to the cabin. "We've got a problem," he announced. "As you know, while we changed the camera positions and lighting to shoot the reverses, we took the horses away for a water break. Unfortunately Rita just noticed that the horses were put back in the wrong order for the reverses. We have to shoot the reverses again."

"Morris, it's almost dark," Lee Chang pointed out. "There's no point in shooting them now. The light will be all wrong."

"I don't care—we're reshooting the reverses. Now." Morris was adamant.

"But it doesn't make sense," Rita told him.

"We're shooting, and that's that," he said. "Come on, come on, let's go." He sounded a little frantic.

By the time we got back to the compound, it was dark. Most of the people involved in the shoot had disappeared into their trailers or headed back to town. I had driven my own car in that morning, but I wanted to see if Bess needed a ride. I knew George would be riding with her mom.

The carpentry shop was closed, and there was no sign of Bess. The whole compound seemed nearly deserted. It was great to see the security lamps on, but they were tuned to the lowest power. Clouds snuck across the moon, and the shadows came and went across my path.

The catering tent had been folded while we'd been at the cabin, and Mrs. Fayne's operation had moved into the original mess hall building. There was no one there but the all-night-coffee-bar guy. He told me that Bess had gone home with George and Mrs. Fayne.

As I circled back toward the parking lot, I was surprised to see Mr. Houseman standing near a large sycamore. I decided to take a minute to thank him for making Mr. Safer's day. I thought that might encourage him to talk to Mr. Safer when he saw him hanging around the compound.

As I approached the tree, I realized Mr. Houseman wasn't aware of me at all. He was deep in conversation with someone who was standing in the shadows and hidden by the tree trunk.

I decided not to interrupt him, but I didn't want him to think I was eavesdropping. So I figured my best move was to just back away quietly.

Step by step I retraced my path, placing each foot carefully onto the ground. I gazed steadily at him as I backed up, but I didn't need to worry about being discovered. He was way too interested in the person in front of him to notice me.

As I watched, he leaned forward to kiss the person in the shadows.

9

Danger in the Dark

I watched the couple for a few minutes. Mr. Houseman's large frame pretty well blocked out the woman he was kissing—I couldn't see her face at all. And it was too dark to identify her by her clothing. They stayed locked in a heavy embrace while I backed away.

I was really careful about not making any noise and revealing myself, and I managed to get out of the area without Mr. Houseman or the mystery woman hearing me. I went to my car and headed for town. The closer I got to home as I drove along the old road, the more I realized how tired I was.

The minute I got home, I called Bess and George and set up a breakfast meeting. George promised that she had news from her data recovery work. I felt like I was falling asleep almost at the same moment I crawled under the covers. I closed my eyes, pushed my pillow into the perfect shape, and barely budged until morning.

I had decided on Susie's Read & Feed café for Thursday breakfast because I wanted privacy while we talked. I especially didn't want anyone from the production company hearing our conversation. And I love Susie's coffee and muffins.

First I told my friends about the problems on the location shoot. Then I described the embrace Mr. Houseman gave the woman in the shadows.

"Wow, who was it, do you think?" Bess asked, her eyes wide.

"It could have been anyone—I didn't see her at all."

"Not Althea," George guessed.

"Probably not," I agreed. "She and Luther seem to be getting very close. But I didn't see the woman, so it's possible."

"It could have been Donnalee, or Rita, or Jane Brandon, or any of the other women in the compound," George said.

"Or it could have been someone from town," I pointed out. "But let's get back to focusing on the sabotage. I've come to the conclusion that it all had to be instigated by someone who knows how the different areas of the production work."

"But that means they have to know when to do these things," Bess said.

"That's what I'm saying," I nodded. "The sabotage has to be perpetrated by someone who not only knows how the different aspects of moviemaking work, but also knows this particular production's schedule."

"Someone on the inside!" Bess said, her eyebrows raising. "Really? Well, I guess that nixes the Muskoka Musketeers and Jack Halloran from the suspect list, doesn't it?" Bess asked.

"Unless Halloran is paying an inside operative to do his dirty work," George muttered, chomping into her egg sandwich.

"Now that the filming has actually begun, things could get really messy around the set," I pointed out. "I need evidence . . . clues . . . *something* that leads us to the culprit. If it's someone on the inside, there's got to be some evidence we can get our hands on. George, you said you have news. I'm hoping you found out something after going through all those computers."

"I did," she said, "but I need more time to trace it. I found the programs that connect to the generators. They were supposed to be loaded on two department's computers: maintenance and security. But there's evidence that a third computer was involved, and the generator program was overwritten with new instructions on that one. I'm tracing its owner."

"So we identify the computer owner, and we might have the saboteur," Bess concluded. She took a bite of her ginger-peach muffin. "But I'd still like to know who's kissing Herman Houseman," Bess added.

"I was going over there to thank him for being so nice to Mr. Safer," I said. "Houseman was pretty kind when I introduced him."

"Don't forget, he's a really good actor," Bess pointed out. "While you were on location, Mr. Safer took a beautiful basket of goodies over to Houseman's trailer. But 'The Great One' brushed him off. Said he was too busy to talk to him."

"Mr. Safer was crushed, right?" George guessed.

"He said he completely understood—but I think it was rude," Bess declared.

"You're right," I agreed. "Just accepting the basket would have been enough to make Mr. Safer happy for days. There really isn't any excuse for deliberately snubbing him like that."

"You know," George said, hesitating for a moment. "There was a computer full of e-mails about meetings. And they were all signed *H*. That could have been Herman. I haven't sorted out who his correspondent is yet, but it won't be long. I keep getting distracted by people wanting help reloading their software."

"Maybe it's his kissing partner," Bess said with a wink.

"Okay, keep at it," I urged. "I'm determined to talk to Jack Halloran. I want to see that script he got. I tried to phone him, but he won't take my calls—and he won't return them either. He knows I heard his fight with Morris and figures my loyalty is with him. But I'll keep after Mr. Halloran—I'll park outside his office if I have to."

"What can I do, Nancy?" Bess asked.

"Just keep your ears and eyes open," I said. "You're right in the thick of the activity, so you're bound to hear all the speculation and rumors. We need to get this case solved soon! I feel like we're sitting on a time bomb."

When we got to the compound, everyone was buzzing about the big scene Herman was about to shoot in the soundstage. It was our first chance to see the great actor at work, so the three of us joined other observers behind the cameras.

Surprisingly, he spent the first hour blanking on lines and bungling cues. "This is absurd," he finally yelled. "I can't recite these lines. They're clearly written by an amateur!"

"Cut!" Morris called.

"Amateur?" Althea bristled. She was standing between Morris and Lee Chang. "Perhaps if the lines were being said by a professional," she continued, "instead of a half-baked *ham* . . ."

At that, Herman turned on his heels and stalked off the set.

"Looks like old Herman's having some trouble with his lines," George whispered. "You'd think someone with all his Broadway experience would be able to remember them better than this."

"Live theater and film are really different for actors," I reminded her in a whisper. "There are a lot of distractions when you're shooting a movie scene—a lot of stopping and starting."

"And sometimes there are stops in the middle of lines," Bess said. "It's hard to keep the flow."

"Keep the flow?" George said. "Give me a break! If you ask me, Herman Houseman's distractions are more personal than professional."

"Are you talking about last night?" I asked.

"I am," George said. "Plus all those e-mails. All I'm saying is he seems to have some whole other agenda aside from making this film."

After a lot of pleading by Morris and Rita, Herman returned. But the scene didn't get any better. Finally Morris yelled "Cut!" for about the fiftieth time. He, Herman, Rita, and Althea all huddled in a loud discussion for a few minutes. Then they left in four different directions.

"I have to get to work," Bess said. "It's afternoon already, and we're trying to get the boat set ready for the big fire scene at ten tonight."

"Why so late?" George asked.

"It probably has something to do with the finance guys Morris is meeting with this evening," I told them.

"Well, I can't play hooky any longer either," George said. "Anybody for supper in a couple of hours?

"Probably not," I said. "I'm going to run a few errands. I'm free until the shoot tonight. I think I'll pay a visit to Harold Safer, and then camp out at Jack Halloran's office."

"Mr. Safer?" Bess asked. "I assume you're after more than just a cheese sandwich."

"I don't know, exactly," I answered. "Just curious about something, I guess. I'll fill you in later, after I talk to him."

My friends went back to work, and I took off in the direction Althea had gone. I wanted her opinion on Mr. Houseman's problems with his lines.

My hunch was right. Althea and Luther were working at one of the rustic picnic tables along the river. It was an absolutely beautiful day—sunny and breezy. A couple dozen Canada geese paddled in formation on the choppy dark Muskoka.

"Nancy!" Luther greeted me. "Come interrupt us. We can use the break."

"Speak for yourself," Althea said with an affection-ate smile for Luther. "I'm really under the gun here." Then she looked at me. Her expression was friendly, but I could tell she hoped I wouldn't interrupt them for too long.

"I only have a minute," I told them, taking a seat at the table. It was littered with white, yellow, blue, ma-genta, and green pages. Each color represented a dif-ferent revision of the script.

"I saw you watching the shoot this morning," Luther said. "What did you think?"

"Funny you should ask," I answered. "That's why I'm here. I'm interested in what you two think is going on with Mr. Houseman."

"He's a jerk," Althea said abruptly, throwing down her pen. "He hasn't learned his lines. He's been in coaching for weeks, and he still stumbles through his part. Now he wants Morris to make up cue cards and have them scattered around the sets, so he can just read them and won't have to memorize anything. Whoever told this guy he could act?"

"Lots of people," Luther said gently. "And you know that. Why he seems unable to demonstrate it on this particular occasion, though, is anybody's guess."

"That's what I'm really curious about," I said. "He's not even close to living up to his reputation. You two are more on the inside than I am. Have you heard any reason why Mr. Houseman's having so much trouble? Is he sick? Any personal problems you know about? Professional problems with Morris or the studio?"

Althea shrugged, and Luther shook his head. "Nancy, we haven't heard anything to explain it," he said. "It's just taking him longer than we all thought it would to adjust to film schedules and the whole moviemaking process, I guess."

"I'm a little harder on the old guy than Luther is," Althea admitted. "I don't think Herman is even *trying* to get it right."

"Well, thanks," I said. "If you do hear anything, let me know. Do you know where Morris is? I'd like to talk to him, too."

"No way you'll get to him right now," Althea warned me. "He's in his office in a meeting with finance people—studio bankers have flown out from the coast. Believe me, you don't want to be even close to that meeting."

"I'm sure you're right," I nodded. "I'll see him later at the fire shoot."

When I left Althea and Luther, I went to my message box in the woman's dressing-room trailer. Crew members left messages there about schedule changes, costume fittings, and script notes. I had only one computer-printed message: *I have information about the so-called accidents on this production, and proof about the canary release! Meet me in the menagerie at seven. Signed, a Friend.*

I've had messages signed "a Friend" before, and that wasn't always an accurate description of the author. But I knew I couldn't ignore it either. I pocketed the note and drove back to town.

First I went to Safer's Cheese Shop. I wanted some quick background on Herman Houseman and figured that Mr. Safer would be my best source of information. I wasn't sure how to approach the subject after Bess's account of his last encounter with the actor. But I didn't have to worry. Mr. Safer brought up the subject the minute I walked into his shop.

"Nancy! I'm so glad you're here!" he said, rushing to greet me. "I can't thank you enough for introducing me to Herman Houseman. It's the highlight of my year by far. What a man! What an actor! And how lucky we are to have him for a while—here in River Heights! It's unbelievable."

"We're very lucky," I said, nodding. "You mentioned seeing him several years ago on Broadway, right?"

"Yes—and what a treat it was! Of course, it was nothing like meeting him in person."

"What has he been doing since you saw him on stage? I believe this is his first film, isn't it?"

"Yes, but only by his choice. He gets dozens of offers and turns them down. And all of them are very lucrative, I might add. He had a sort of slow period for a few years, but then it was as if he'd been discovered all over again—the offers began pouring in. Especially lately. Probably because of his triumph in *Long Day's Journey into Night,* his star has never been higher. People are clamoring for his talent, and paying dearly to get it. His agent can practically auction him off to the highest bidder."

We chatted a little more, and then I left. Mr. Safer had no answer for the puzzle I had to solve: If Herman Houseman was being offered a ton of money for all these other jobs, what was he doing on a low-budget production like *Stealing Thunder?*

From the cheese shop I went straight to Rackham Industries. I was determined to see the script that made Jack Halloran so angry. When I told his secretary that I wasn't leaving until he saw me, she finally ushered me into his office.

"What is it, Nancy?" Mr. Halloran barked from behind his desk. "If you're here to plead the case for *Stealing Thunder* and Morris Dunnowitz, you're wasting your breath. I've made up my mind to fight that production to the finish."

"I'm not here to argue with you," I said. "I want to know just want one thing. Who sent you the script?"

"I don't know. It was dropped off here at the office—I assume by a courier. Why?"

"May I see it?"

"I guess so." He reached into a desk drawer and pulled out a plain manila envelope and handed it to me. I skimmed through it, jumping from scene to scene.

"Mr. Halloran, this isn't the screenplay for *Stealing Thunder*. I don't know who wrote this, but this is *not* the script we're shooting."

He grabbed it back. "What do you mean?" he asked. "It has to be."

"But it's not. I'm playing your ancestor Esther Rackham, and I'm very familiar with the script. Someone has pulled a major hoax here, and I'm afraid you're the victim. Because of that, I'm sure I can persuade Morris and Althea Waters, the screenwriter, to let you read the correct version. I think you'll see there are no lies or distortions in it. You know that Luther Eldridge would not be consulting if there were!"

Mr. Halloran studied my face hard, as if he was trying to bore right into my brain and see if I was telling the truth. "All right, if you can set it up, I'll read the real screenplay."

"Deal," I said.

By the time I got back to the compound, it was six

forty-five. The sun had set, but the sky still glowed with a dull dusky light. The air was cool, so I zipped a red sweatshirt on over my jeans and T-shirt.

I walked around the soundstage to the menagerie. The horses were still outside, in a pen next to the stable. They whinnied at my arrival and ran in circles a couple of times. They seemed restless—maybe they knew there was a shoot in a couple of hours.

I looked around for Jake, but there was no one near the place, so I selected a spot bathed in bright light from a portable security lamp and sat down on a stump to wait for "a Friend."

Seven o'clock . . . a quarter after. Still no one came, and there was no sign of Jake. The horses were really restless by then, and they were still circling the perimeter of the pen. The pale light was gone from the sky by that time, and everything looked gray.

I started to feel a little jittery myself. I walked over to pat a couple of the horses and maybe calm them—and me—down. But they jumped back, and one reared on his hindlegs and snorted.

A low noise caught my attention. I followed the sound about thirty yards over to the trailer Jake had shown us—the temporary home of mountain lions Kaia and Thunder. "So *that's* why the horses are nervous," I muttered to myself. "I can't believe Jake would leave one of the cats out here all by itself."

But he had. Thunder was pacing back and forth against the wall of the huge cage. A high metal roof kept him inside, but he was clearly not happy. "Hey, fella, where's your pal?" I said to the cat, in my most soothing tone. "Jake? Hey, Jake. Where are you?" I knocked on the trailer door, but there was no answer, and it didn't budge.

I wasn't really afraid of the lion. It was a trained animal, and used to people. But I was still cautious—after all, I wasn't his trainer. So I hung back about five or six feet from the cage and tried to comfort the restless cat.

"Thunder, be cool," I murmured. "Jake will be back soon, I'm sure. Just settle down, boy. I'll wait here with you. We can just hang out—"

It happened so fast, it was like a streaking meteor—you see it, and then it's gone. Thunder crouched back, bared his teeth, and pounced. He hit the cage so hard that the door popped open. And the strength of his leap vaulted him straight at me.

10

What's My Motivation?

T **hunder flew at me** in a tawny streak. Instinctively I dove toward the right, shielding my head with my arms.

The lion sailed over my body and landed with a soft *thruuump* in the grass. In an instant he was out of sight.

For a few seconds I was overcome by a flood of tremors. When they finally stopped, I punched in the autodial key on my cell that connected me to the security trailer. I told Dave Linn what had happened, and he and Jane were there in minutes.

"We've got to find Jake," I told them. While Dave searched around the menagerie area, Jane entered the combination into the trailer lock. We found Jake tied up inside. He was conscious, but he had a nasty bump on the back of his head. He didn't remember what had happened—only that he'd been knocked out from behind.

Jake refused to go to the on-site doctor's office, and insisted on going after Thunder immediately. He, Jane, and Dave rode two horses and a security van off toward the woods in the same direction as the running Thunder. By the time Chief McGinnis of the police arrived, the posse had already returned, with Thunder safely locked in the van. Jake transferred the cat into its "room" in the trailer, and then finally went to get checked out by the doctor.

"Well, my job here is done," Chief McGinnis announced. He often does that—takes credit for the work that others do. But I let him get away with it, because he's an excellent source in the River Heights Police Department, and he often helps me on cases—sometimes unintentionally.

"I'm going to turn in a report to Morris," Jane said when the menagerie had finally calmed down for the night. "Do you want to come?"

"I'll be along in a few minutes," I told her. "I have to get changed for the fire scene."

I was going to wait until Jake got back from the doctor's office, but I just couldn't. I had to examine that outdoor cage. He had bragged about how secure it was. If so, why did the door pop open when

Thunder lunged at the cage wall? It had all been so fast, I hadn't really seen what had happened.

I went back to get a closer look at the door. Amazingly, it was still locked shut. It had been the hinged side that had broken away. I examined the door closely, and confirmed my suspicion. The door had been hanging by a thread—a screw thread.

The original hinge screws had been removed and replaced with ones that had been filed down. Everything looked fine if you just looked at the screw heads on the surface—but you could pull them out easily, without using a screwdriver. One jolt against the door, and the screws popped right out.

I carefully picked up a couple of the screws with a tissue and placed them in my pocket. My fingers glided against the message from "a Friend." I'd almost forgotten why I was in the menagerie in the first place. I wondered, was I lured to the area by the same person who filed down the hinge screws? If so, someone thought I was a lot closer to solving this case than *I* did.

I went to the dressing-room trailer and pulled on my blue homespun dress with the flowered shawl. With a quick touchup of my makeup by Pam and Degas, I was ready. I had an hour until my call, but I decided to go to the soundstage early and watch Bess help with the set. I was eager to tell her about my near miss with Thunder.

Speaking of near misses—if I had only left the makeup trailer just a *little* earlier, I would not have had to hear my name spoken by that dreaded voice. "Well, Nan-cy Drew," Deirdre Shannon said. "What on earth are *you* doing out here?"

I wanted to run, but instead, I turned. "Hello, Deirdre. I might ask you the same question."

She was dressed in a low-cut black cocktail dress and was teetering in the dirt on spike sandals. Crystal chandeliers hung from her earlobes, sparkling incongruously in the wilderness moonlight. We must have made an interesting sight—a pioneer woman and a party chick.

"I'm here to audition for the film being shot in River Heights. You probably don't know anything about that, though. Are you helping out the caterer? I hear your friend's mother is doing the food." She looked at my dress, and her nose wrinkled slightly. "Odd waitress uniforms," she observed. "Or are you a dishwasher?"

"Easy, DeeDee. I've already been attacked by one cat tonight." I've known Deirdre for my whole life— since we were kids in school—and being around her never gets any better. She's totally obnoxious, and more in love with herself than anyone I know.

"Do you know anything about the movie?" she asked.

"Yes. I'm in the cast, actually." I hate to admit it, but I *loved* the expression on her face when that sunk in. "I'm surprised it took you so long to get out here. We've been shooting for days."

"Who's in charge here?" she asked curtly. "Where should I go for an audition?"

"I'll tell you what," I said, steering her toward Herman Houseman's trailer. "Why don't you just check in over there. I'm sure the gentlemen inside will be happy to help you."

Deirdre marched over and knocked on the door. I couldn't leave—I had to see how Mr. Houseman would react when yet another River Heights citizen knocked on his private trailer.

The door opened a crack and Deirdre talked for a few moments with the person inside. Then she spun around and stormed down the steps. I suppressed my giggle as she teetered back over to me. "That wasn't the right place at all—as you probably know. It's that building over there—the office. And I thought you were rude, but the woman in that trailer could give you lessons!" She brushed by me and wobbled toward the office.

I didn't waste my time imagining Deirdre crashing Morris's meeting with the bankers—I was struck by something she said. Who was the rude *woman* in Herman's trailer? Could it have been the woman he had kissed the night before? I had to find out. I crouched behind a nearby tree and watched the front of the trailer. At last the door opened again. Out stepped Rita Clocker. Before she left, Mr. Houseman arrived. I could tell by the way they touched in passing that Rita was the kissing woman.

Before I could straighten from my observation crouch, I felt a tap on my shoulder. I turned and looked into my favorite pair of brown eyes—the ones belonging to my boyfriend, Ned Nickerson. He kissed me before I could speak.

"Hi there," I said. "What are you doing here? I thought you were still in Chicago for that book fair."

"Nah, I missed you too much and decided to come home early. Besides, I heard you were almost lion lunch and figured you might need some protection."

"Wait just a minute. How did you find out about that?"

"I called the office up here to let you know I was home early, but no one was taking calls over there. So I called the next best thing: the mess hall. Boy, was I surprised when George answered! I didn't know Mrs. Fayne had gotten this account. Anyway, George filled me in on everything that's happened. Some of her story sounded more like a movie than real life."

"You have no idea," I told him. "I can't wait to tell

you all about it. Come on, you can watch us shoot the fire scene."

"Wait a minute. I have a present for you. I picked it up in Chicago. You're going to love it." He reached into his book bag and pulled out a flashy-looking magazine. "It's a Hollywood gossip sheet," he explained. "And it's got a big article about your costar Herman Houseman. I don't usually buy this stuff, of course, but *this* issue . . . well, wait till you read it."

I was thrilled. I definitely needed another assessment of Herman Houseman besides Harold Safer's. Ned and I found a quiet place near a security light, and sat down to comb the pages of *Hollywood Heartbreak*.

It turns out that Mr. Safer was closer to the truth than I gave him credit for. The article said that Mr. Houseman had received a big offer from a major Hollywood producer but Morris's attorneys had him in an airtight contract for another film.

"'But take heart, Houseman fans,'" I read aloud, "'Herman says he has just a few more things to take care of and then he'll be able to sign the new contract!'"

"The article says that the new movie begins filming in one week," Ned explained. It seemed that they were going to cast someone else in the romantic lead if

Herman couldn't get released from his contract for *Stealing Thunder*. Apparently, they were guaranteeing him a million dollars up front, percentages, bonuses. It was the role of a lifetime . . . in more ways than one.

11

Take Two

Motive!" I whispered. "**We** finally have someone who has a *real* motive for shutting down this production. Come on!"

I still had a half hour before I had to report to the set. Ned and I raced across the compound to the mess hall and found George. We showed her the magazine, and I summarized the article about Herman Houseman.

"Motive!" she cried.

"Exactly," I said. "Can you get away for a few minutes?"

"Absolutely." She checked out with her mother and returned to Ned and me.

"I want all the dirt you can get me on Rita

Clocker," I told George. "She's the woman Herman was kissing last night."

"Yeah? I had my money on Donnalee," George said. "Come on."

She took us to the office, and the room in which she'd untangled all the computer data. It didn't take long to find out what we wanted—especially once George snuck into the studio database and Rita's employment file. All for the sake of the case, of course.

"There she is," George announced. "Whoa, we've even got her fingerprints."

"Excellent," I said. Then I told my friends what I had discovered about the hinges on Thunder's cage door.

"Nancy, that could have been bad," George pointed out.

"Not really," I said. "I believe Jake when he said that Thunder wasn't really after me. He just wanted a romp in the woods. When they went out there to get him, Thunder walked up to the van the first time Jake called him."

I didn't tell them the rest of what Jake had said— about how Thunder was still a wild animal, and if he'd decided that I would've made a good wrestling partner, he could have tossed me around like a rag doll. No need to worry my friends, right?

"Hel–lo, what have we here?" George pulled my attention back to the computer screen. "Check this out."

"That's Rita's address in Hollywood, right?" Ned asked.

"It is. Now look at this."

"Herman's address," I said as I read. "And they're the same! I knew it. Those two are definitely a couple."

"And the couple that plots together—," George began.

"Splits a million-dollar signing fee, plus percentages, plus bonuses, together," Ned finished.

"Okay, Morris, you're going to *have* to meet with me now," I declared. "Where's his meeting?"

"In the conference room," George answered. "It's just like this room, but on the opposite side of the building."

"Wish me luck," I told them.

"Luck," Ned echoed, with a thumbs–up sign.

"Can we come?" George begged.

"Wait for me in the lobby and send me mental cheers when I barge in."

"Done," she said.

They followed me into the small reception lobby, which was empty. "His assistant and the office girl are both in there with him," George explained.

"Great," I said. "Nobody to tackle me before I barge in."

I stood outside the conference-room door. Then I took a deep breath and opened it.

"Go get 'em," Ned whispered.

There were six visitors in the room—four men and two women. They and the office employees looked startled. Morris looked positively stunned.

"Na-Na-Nancy!" he stammered. "As you can see I'm very busy at the moment. We can talk at another time."

"Excuse me for interrupting you, Morris, but this can't wait. I need to talk to you now."

"But I'm—"

"I realize you're busy, but I *really* need to talk to you."

"Very well," he said. He'd lost his initial shock, and was beginning to sound irritated. "Everyone, please take a few minutes' break. Help yourself to refreshments."

Morris followed me to the reception lobby, where George and Ned were waiting, and shut the door behind him.

"This had better be an emergency," he said, his teeth clamped. "I was close to closing the deal in there."

"You don't want to make a deal without this information," I assured him. "Prepare yourself—I'm pretty sure Herman Houseman and Rita Clocker are partners behind the sabotage that's been perpetrated against this production."

"What?! You're not serious. Are you serious?"

I didn't even let him think about it. I just peppered him with speculations, deductions, and conclusions.

"Have you heard about the movie deal Herman's been offered?" I asked.

"Sure, but I don't believe it," Morris said. "It's just a trick by his agent to try to wring more money out of me."

I showed him the article, with the quotes from the producers of the new movie.

"I know that producer," Morris said. "He would never let his name be used unless the facts were right. I don't believe this."

I told him about Rita and Herman living together, and about seeing them kiss the night before. "Who better than the continuity chief to guarantee that the production goes way over budget? Think how much money we lost just on the day the reverses were bungled," I pointed out. "And that was an outright continuity error. Plus, in her job she had access to pratically all the keys and locks in the compound," I added.

"George is close to bringing us the hard evidence we need—the e-mails from Herman and the address of the recipient. I'm sure that we'll find that Rita's computer was the third one programmed to run the generators," I concluded. "How she got her hands on it will be an amazing story, I'm sure."

"She's very computer literate," George said. "I've realized that since my first day on the job. If she's not good enough to disable all the machines herself, she's at least good enough to hire someone to do the job and explain what she wants done."

"And the food poisoning?" Morris asked.

"She was probably behind that, too," I said, "but it might be hard to prove. We should have enough information to put them away for quite a while, though." I told him about the cage door hinge screws.

"That could have been a real disaster," Morris said.

"They were getting desperate, I think," I told him. "Apparently, they knew I was closing in before I did."

"Yikes!" Morris yelled, checking his watch. "We have to get to the soundstage."

"Relax, boss," George said. "They can't start without you."

"But they can," he protested. "I told my assistant director to start the shoot because I didn't know how long I'd be tied up with the potential backers. If Rita and Herman have something planned for this scene, it really *will* be a disaster!"

He tore out of the building and ran to the soundstage. We followed.

"I don't get it," Ned said, racing with us. "Why is this scene so risky?"

"It's the moment when Ethan Mahoney, played by Houseman, is knocked out by the Rackham brothers during the robbery," I explained between gasps. "He's in his office on the houseboat, and they set fire to it as a parting shot. Ethan regains consciousness, puts out the fire, and limps off the boat to get help."

"Luther talked the River Heights Museum into letting us use a bunch of authentic artifacts to dress the set," George continued.

"We're setting a real fire—*briefly*," Morris called back over his shoulder. "If they try to sabotage this shoot and hundreds of thousands of artifacts go up in smoke—trust me, it'll be a disaster. We'll lose our insurance coverage and have to close down for good."

As we reached the soundstage, I told the others to go ahead while I called Chief McGinnis. When I finally stepped inside, I looked around for our two suspects. Herman was onstage, running through his lines, but I didn't see Rita anywhere on the scene. Then she entered from stage left. She was carrying an old-fashioned fire extinguisher. She walked across the set to where another extinguisher was hanging on the wall. She took the one off the wall and placed it on the floor—then she substituted the one she was carrying, hanging it on the wall instead.

12

Action!

I followed Rita to a spot just off the set. When her back was turned to answer a question, I grabbed the extinguisher she had removed from the wall. It was heavy. Then I checked the one she had substituted. It was feather-light—so light it had to be empty. I switched the two extinguishers back the way they had been.

"All right, everyone. Are we ready?" Morris's assistant director yelled. "Are the backups ready?" To be safe, six men and women, all armed with extinguishers, skirted the set out of camera range. "All right, then. Here we go. Action!"

The scene began with the fire. Herman, as Ethan Mahoney, lay on the floor. Then he groaned and rolled up onto his knees. Shaking his head, his expression changed to panic at the prospect of his houseboat going up in flames. He staggered to the wall, rubbing the back of his head. He pulled down the extinguisher and turned the hose onto the fire.

When the retardant shot out of the hose, Houseman seemed to lose character for a moment and be genuinely surprised. He aimed it at the flames, and they were extinguished quickly.

"Cut! Print!"

"*Police!* Don't anybody move!"

At first everyone thought it was part of the movie. But I recognized Chief McGinnis's voice. He barged onto the set, pushing Ben and Luke Alvarez in ahead of him, their hands in the air. He held them at gunpoint with a triumphant expression. Two of his officers followed. Apparently the guns and masks the guys were wearing as the Rackham Gang persuaded Chief McGinnis they were real thieves—real thieves who dressed in eccentric costumes.

"Is this some sort of sting?" Luke asked, his voice muffled by the bandanna mask he had tied around his mouth for the next take.

"Or is this a joke, Morris?" Ben asked. "I promise, I'll learn my lines. I get your point!"

"Chief McGinnis, thank you for arriving so promptly," I said, walking over to stand beside him. I needed to help him save face. "That was a brilliant way to sneak undetected onto the set. Now you can let Luke and Ben go and arrest the real culprits."

Chief McGinnis seemed confused, until I pointed to Rita and Herman. A collective gasp fluttered around the set as the officers handcuffed the two. Morris explained to the rest of the crowd that they were being accused of the sabotage that had plagued the company since it arrived. I recounted the same arguments that I had used earlier to convince Morris.

"And I believe that if you compare the fire extinguisher that Herman just used to the one near where Rita is standing," I added, "you'll see that the two had planned one last devastating attack on this production. And it was one that could have resulted in more than just lost artifacts and lost insurance. If the fire had gotten out of control, it could have caused someone's death."

"But the one I used was full," Herman protested.

"Yes, that was the one I specifically hung on the wall just before we started shooting," Rita said with a smug look.

"I'm afraid not," I told her, explaining how I'd reversed her switch.

"So you apparently have all the answers," Houseman said.

"Except a couple," I answered him. "About Muriel and Thunder—which of you released the bird

149

and filed down the screws in the mountain lion's cage?"

"We shared those honors," Houseman said. "Rita shooed the bird away, and I personally loosened the hinges so that the slightest pressure by Thunder on the door would release it. Having you in front of the door when it opened," he cooed, "was a bonus."

The officers escorted Rita and Herman off the set. I was happy to have Bess arrive in time to see them leave.

"You can let those two go," Morris told the chief, pointing to Ben and Luke. "They've got a robbery to commit!"

For a moment Chief McGinnis didn't say anything. I couldn't tell if he was confused or embarrassed. Then suddenly he joined with the others in a round of laughter and applause.

Right on cue, Harold Safer walked in with a large platter of cheese and fruit. "Thank you for the applause," he said, with a slight blush. "But this is just our regular weekly special—nothing overly fancy."

"We're applauding because Nancy solved the mystery of who's been sabotaging this movie production," Ned told Mr. Safer. "And the culprits have already been taken away by the police."

"Wonderful," Mr. Safer said. "And who were the creeps?"

"I'm sorry to have to tell you," I said. "One of them was Rita Clocker."

"That nice woman I met in the mess tent?" Harold said with a surprised look. "My, you certainly can't judge a book by its cover, can you?"

"No, you can't," I agreed, biting my lip. I hated to tell him the next part. "The second criminal was Herman Houseman."

"No!" Harold said. "You can't be serious! Not a wonderful actor like Mr. Houseman!"

He sank onto one of the benches in the houseboat set. His face looked as white as the doilies on his cheese-and-fruit platter.

"Well, we're not only through shooting for the night," Morris called to the cast and crew. "We might be through shooting *period*. Our understudy quit yesterday, but I thought we were safe. Without an Ethan Mahoney, the film is truly doomed."

"Nancy Drew, Headhunter, reporting for duty," I said. It sounded kind of silly, so I added a goofy smile.

"Okay, Nancy, you're on," Morris said. "You've been batting a thousand so far. Who've you got in mind?"

"You already thought of him once yourself," I answered, nodding toward Harold Safer.

"Me?" Mr. Safer asked.

Tripp, Julie, Degas, and Pam closed in on Harold,

circling him the way a gardener looks at a topiary. "We can definitely do this," Tripp announced to Morris.

"We can make him look like Herman Houseman, we can make him look like Ethan Mahoney," Degas stated. "Whatever you want."

"Houseman completed only one of his scenes," I reminded Morris. "It won't cost that much to reshoot."

"All right," Morris finally said. "What have we got to lose? Go do your magic," he told the wardrobe and makeup teams. "Make me a believer."

The four artisans carted Mr. Safer across the set. Before they left the room, Morris called out one final question. "Tell me, Harold—have you ever acted? Do you know anything about the stage and movies?

The pink surged back into Harold's white cheeks. "Do I?" he called out triumphantly. "Most definitely. Action!"

She's sharp.

She's smart.

She's confident.

She's unstoppable.

And she's on your trail.

MEET THE NEW NANCY DREW

Still sleuthing,

still solving crimes,

but she's got some new tricks up her sleeve!

NANCY DREW

girl detective

star power

by Catherine Hapka

power

She's beautiful, she's talented, she's famous.

She's a star!

Things would be perfect
if only her family
was around to help
her celebrate. . . .

Follow the
adventures of
fourteen-year-old
pop star
Star Calloway